Hope you enjoy it,
Catherine

Ruth Daigneault

The 13th Guest

RUTH S. DAIGNEAULT

Also by Ruth S. Daigneault

Novels

The Queen's Spy

Non-Fiction

The Last Journey - Going Home
(With L. Paul Daigneault)

Writing as Ruth S. Rogers
Fifteen Dinner Theatre Comedy Plays including

The Grand Reopening of Cin's Saloon

The Wedding

Whispering Pines

S. S. Gigantic

The Pink Flamingo

This book is a work of fiction. All the characters, names and situations

are the product of the author's imagination. Any resemblance to any actual events, locales or persons, living or dead, is coincidental.

First Printing - BookBaby August 2016

The 13th Guest by Ruth S. Daigneault

ISBN 978-0-9918053-7-2

With love to my husband, Paul, and

my children, Debbie, Heather and Tony.

Special thanks to Paul, who allowed me to take his story, Restless Diva, change it around to suit my purposes and use it in the book.

CONTENTS

Chapter 1

THE HOSTS

"God, I hate this thing!" Leona Beckworth said, swatting aside the skeleton hanging in the doorway. It partially blocked her view and she very much wanted to see what was going on at the bottom of their walkway where her uncle seemed to be having some kind of debate with two strangers.

The skeleton brushed the top of her husband's head. Derek swore under his breath and glared at his wife as he steadied the bones and stepped around them.

Colonel Thomas Montgomery's gloved right hand extended out from the arm of a beige trench coat to make a variety of circles in the air. His head bobbed around and although his words were indistinguishable, the conversation appeared animated. The listeners were a man and woman who had alighted from a taxi. The young woman looked all around at the grounds and up to the second floor of the large brick house.

The Colonel's normally rigid back was rounded as he bent forward toward the others. The man patted his back in a gesture of reassurance. After considerable head-nodding and arm swinging from the old soldier, he straightened up and all three turned toward the steps, still talking. The words "...will be fine" carried up to Derek and Leona.

"Is everything all right?" Derek asked as he looked from one to the other.

The Colonel cleared his throat and waved his hand in dismissal. "Yes. Perfectly. Just a minor problem with the cabbie - nothing to worry about." He pushed his glasses higher on his nose and cleared his throat again. "These are my friends I told you about, Joe Walters and Laura Carter. My niece, Leona, and her husband, Derek."

Derek extended his hand. "Welcome to spooky tales night at the humble Beckworth home." The men shook hands, Laura gave a brief smile but did not meet their eyes.

Leona took in the granny glasses barely visible above the collar of the plain wool coat and decided Derek's wandering eye would pass on by. "The butler will take your coats," she said. "Please have a drink and make yourselves comfortable."

"I'll see that they get settled," Thomas said, ushering the couple inside.

Leona watched them disappear and made a disparaging sound. "That woman must have bought her clothes at a second-hand shop." Her brow furrowed. "I wonder what that commotion was all about. I can't imagine what kind of problem the cab driver would give them."

"Hmmm. Yes. Rather odd," Derek said. "As to the couple, they look somewhat young to be Thomas' friends."

"You know he likes to have young people around, and speaking of friends, remember what I told you earlier." Leona's voice grew cold and her brown eyes darkened. "Keep your hands off Angie tonight. It's bad enough that I know you sneak around with her, but I will not have you flaunting it in my face in front of guests."

"Are you on that again?! I thought we settled that this afternoon." Derek sighed deeply and turned away.

Angie grabbed his shoulder and spun him around. "It would be settled if I believed you ... which I don't."

Derek flung his hands out. "For God's sake, I've told you more than once, we're not having an affair."

"Right." Leona folded her arms across her chest

Derek rolled his eyes. "Just drop it, will you? This is a party and I don't need your stupid and unfounded jealousy wrecking it."

"If you keep your hands to yourself, there won't be a problem."

Derek stepped outside and lit a cigarette. *Damn Leona! She was getting too suspicious. I'll have to be more careful.*

He shoved his hand in his pocket, tipped his head back and watched a long trail of smoke head to the sky. He closed his eyes, thought of Angie and smiled. A flash of light penetrated his eyelids. Derek looked toward the street and saw headlights approaching their drive. *If this happens to be Brent and Angie ... bad timing, with Leona already in a foul mood.* He threw away his cigarette and went back inside.

Chapter 2

THE GUESTS

The music from Sirius played softly on the car radio. Brent didn't hear it. His mind was elsewhere, divided between peering through the darkness at the road and thinking about his life. More accurately, his wife. After eight years of marriage, he was fed up with her spending habits, not to mention her drinking. Brent risked a quick glance at her. She was as beautiful at 44 as she had been when they married, as well she should be, he thought, given the amount of time she spent at spas and beauty clinics. He suspected all those treatments weren't for his benefit.

Waves of long blonde hair fell over Angie's shoulders as she leaned back against the seat. "I hope Derek has a decent Scotch on hand," she said.

Brent sighed. "I'm sure his bar will be well-stocked, Angie. But it wouldn't hurt you to lay off the booze a little."

"It's a party, for God's sake. People are supposed to drink."

"I know that. But ..."

"Come on, Brent. You wouldn't deny me a little drinkie, would you?" she cooed and leaned her head on his shoulder.

"Your little girl talk is getting thin, Angie."

She gritted her teeth. *Damn, sometimes Brent is a pain in the ass. No, make that a LOT of the time. If only Derek would make a move and get a divorce from Leona.* That thought reminded her of something she wanted to know but couldn't very well ask Derek.

She lifted her head, sat back, pulled out a cigarette case and a lighter. "Do you think Derek's diamond mine is as big a hit as he says it is?"

"Apparently. There seems to be no end to the original huge vein discovered two years ago." Brent stole a quick look at her. "Why do you ask?"

"Just curious. I'm sure Derek's glad not to have to depend on Leona's money any more." The gold lighter shimmered in the light of the flame as Angie lit her cigarette.

Brent frowned. "Open your window. You know I can't stand the smoke."

"It's cold out there." Brent said nothing. Angie muttered an oath, but complied.

"As to Derek being independent from Leona's money, I'm not so sure. I believe she's heavily invested in the mine. And it's Derek's fault that he wasted the money he received when Colin died, although I guess part of that could be blamed on Leona. She's always been a spendthrift. They've never lacked for anything."

Angie pulled the fur collar higher against the draft. "Except love, maybe," she said under her breath.

"What?"

"Nothing." Angie leaned her head against the plush headrest again and sighed. She remained silent until she reached over to stub out her cigarette in the ash tray and close the window.

Angie blew out a long breath and Brent tried not to inhale the alcohol fumes that refused to be smothered by her Chanel perfume or the smell of the cigarette smoke which tried to find a way out through the roof..

The approach to the sprawling Beckworth estate on the outskirts of Ottawa was a tunnel of tall elm trees which formed a canopy over the long driveway in the summertime. But on this breezy October night, the barren limbs were scrabbling at the sky as if trying to grab the dark gown with their spindly fingers. Huge willows, branches drooping in mourning, completed the eerie scene which somehow befitted All Hallow's Eve. Angie spotted Derek standing on the porch, said nothing as she watched him go back inside..

A taxi moved away from the front entrance as Brent drove up, and a white-gloved valet hurried to open the door for Angie. Brent took her arm as they made their way up the steps. Grimacing pumpkins on either side of the stairs watched their progress through eyes that flickered with a yellow light. A luminescent skeleton swung lazily in the centre of the doorway, its bones rattling as Brent and Angie pushed through to enter the foyer where their hosts were waiting.

Derek's light gray slacks were set off by a white turtleneck showing under a dark blue blazer. If he was trying to achieve a freshman look, Brent thought, he nearly succeeded. His 6'4" frame was still athletic. The only telltale signs of a more senior age were the graying goatee and mustache, and a hairline which was definitely sliding backwards.

Brent extended his hand. "Derek! Nice to see you."

Derek slapped Brent on the shoulder. "Glad you could make it buddy. It's going to be a special night." He turned to Angie. "Nice to see you, Angie."

The top of her head just past his chin, Angie inhaled his familiar Clive Christian aftershave and pressed herself against Derek in a long hug. "I wouldn't miss it for the world, Derek." The fur of her mink coat tickled his neck and he rubbed it briefly when she stepped back.

Leona Beckworth glared at Angie then turned to give Brent a perfunctory hug causing her long, form-fitting, green satin evening dress to ripple and glisten.

Brent pressed his lips briefly on her cheek. He drew back and looked into her eyes. "You're looking lovely, as always, Leona."

The two women kissed the air by each other's cheeks. Angie did a mental calculation on how much Leona's diamond necklace was worth and a count of the wrinkles in her neck. Leona decided she would have to think of something to stop Angie in her tracks.

"I hope you two have your stories ready," Derek said.

Leona rolled her eyes. "Men," she muttered.

Brent and Angie left the hosts and Angie grabbed a drink from a waiter as they entered the drawing room, disturbing some of the ghosts that floated from the ceiling by nearly-invisible filaments. The vast size of the room was softened by the multiple arrangements of comfortable chairs and polished tables. The marble mantlepiece held family photographs lined up on either side of a large urn, its base consumed by greedy fingers of flames reflected from the blazing fire below. Lamps with orange bulbs added a healthy hue to the faces of the guests already gathered.

Colonel Montgomery stood to the side of the fireplace recounting rather loudly his glory days before, during and after the Gulf War to a bored-looking young man perched on the arm of a green chair. Catching sight of Brent, he jumped up and called out, cutting off Colonel Montgomery in mid-sentence.

"Brent!"

Not to be deterred, the old soldier turned and began talking to his friends and the pretty blonde seated with them. Her attention was focussed on the young man who had just left to talk to Brent.

Brent smiled, clapped his left hand on Peter's shoulder and extended the other. "Peter! Glad you could make it."

"Very happy to be here. And this lovely lady must be your wife." He smiled warmly at the woman whose eyes gleamed in appreciation.

"Right you are. Angie, this is the new law partner I told you about, Peter Morrison. My wife, Angie."

Angie smiled warmly at the tall young man. "What brings you to our nation's capital?" Angie said, "Politics? Scandal?"

Peter laughed. "Neither of those. I think the most honest answer would be ... a job."

"Well, I hope you like it here," Angie said. She placed her empty glass on the tray being offered to them by a waiter in a pirate costume and helped herself to another.

Derek entered the room and looked around.

"Please excuse me," Angie said, carelessly pushing her hair off her shoulder..

Both men watched her walk off toward Derek, Brent's eyes thoughtful, Peter's admiring the way her hips swayed under the clingy black material of her dress. *Lucky man.*

Peter saw the look on his friend's face and decided a change of subject was needed. "I guess there are going to be quite a few people here this evening," he said.

Brent returned his attention to Peter. "Oh, uh, yes. An even dozen, so Derek told me. A small number, really, for a place this size."

"True." Peter looked around. "Taxes must be a fortune." He sipped his drink.

"Let's just say I wouldn't want to foot the bill," Brent said. "How is your mother? I haven't seen Helen since she and Michael won that lottery and moved up north."

"She's fine, physically. Still trying to get over Dad's disappearance."

"Right. When was that? A couple of years ago?"

"About that." Peter sighed. "She still hasn't come to terms with Dad being gone. I think she expects him to walk in the door any minute."

"That's too bad. What happened there exactly? I only saw a brief mention in the paper."

"Well, not that I don't want to tell you," Peter said, "but as we had to come up with some kind of scary story tonight, I thought I'd tell that as my contribution."

Brent nodded. "Oh, of course. Good idea. And your sister, Amy? Is she still with your Mom?"

"No, Amy moved to Chicago a few years before Dad disappeared - following the love of her life, I understand. She was pretty upset over Dad though and came back to stay with Mom for a while, but then she went back to Chicago. I haven't seen her in ages."

"Well, I'd recognize that flaming red hair anywhere," Brent laughed. "She'd certainly stand out in a crowd."

Peter laughed too. "Very true. I could always spot her in the schoolyard when we were kids." He lowered his voice. "By the way, thank you for rescuing me from the old fellow."

"He can be a bit of a bore," Brent agreed, "although he's not really that old. About sixty-five, I would guess. He's Leona's uncle - Colonel Montgomery. I think he was her guardian when she was younger. At least he was the trustee who guarded her money."

Brent glanced around the room. There was no sign of the Colonel - or Angie and Derek. "I see he's gone. Must have finally decided to deprive Kelly and those other two of the pleasure of his company." They chuckled.

The men thanked the hovering waiter as they helped themselves to a drink.

"What about George? Is he working somewhere?"

Peter raised his eyebrows and shook his head. "I have no idea where George is or what he's doing. He just seemed to vanish into thin air after Dad disappeared. Not that he was around much beforehand either."

"Really? Sad sometimes how families lose touch with each other." Brent sipped his drink. "Have you met everyone, Peter?"

"No. I didn't have a chance. The colonel jumped me as soon as I came in."

"Come on and I'll introduce you to Kelly Jamieson, and we'll both find out who those other two are, now that Montgomery has released them from his clutches. Judging by her plain outfit, I'm guessing the lady's a teacher or a librarian. Maybe it's just those glasses that make me think that."

"Appearances can be deceiving, Brent, but in this case, I agree."

"Let's see how wrong we are." Brent smiled. As they headed over to the threesome, Brent saw Angie return alone and lighten the load of a passing waiter's tray.

"Kelly, nice to see you again," Brent said. "I'd like to introduce you to Peter Morrison, newest member of Richardson, Maguire, etc. law firm. Peter, this is Kelly Jamieson, soon to be rich and famous, artist."

"Really, Mr. Richardson. You exaggerate, as always," Kelly said, looking pleased, "although since Derek commissioned me to do his portrait, I've been contacted by five more families." She looked at the younger man, smiled and offered her hand. "Nice to meet you Peter."

"My pleasure I'm sure," Peter said, his blue eyes sparkling. He held her hand just a little longer than necessary. "You do portraits?"

"Yes, among other things. The Beckworths have a room full of family portraits dating back a couple of hundred years and Mr. Richards," her short blonde curly hair bounced when she nodded toward Brent, "was kind enough to recommend me to Derek as the person to paint his."

"I swear, Kelly, I'll be dancing at your wedding some day and you'll still be calling me Mr. Richardson."

Kelly laughed and tapped his arm. "I can't help it. You've been Mr. Richardson since grade school choir practice. Just cause I'm fifteen years older now ..."

"Ugh! Please don't remind me." Brent turned inquiringly to the couple beside Kelly.

"Joe Walters," the man said, extending his hand. "And my friend and assistant, Laura Carter." Laura nodded and turned her head slightly, causing her long, black hair to fall further over her face. 'We're friends of Colonel Montgomery."

All heads turned at the sound of a squeal in the doorway.

"Ooooh, look. Carmen. Isn't this just tooooo spooky."

"Wow! That's Dani Davis, isn't it?" Kelly whispered.

"In the flesh," Laura said. "Obviously."

Danielle Davis was a buxom redhead, with a figure that would ignite the passion in any man, and had done so countless times, if her box office appeal was any indication. She smiled confidently and accepted the admiring glances as her due. The lights bounced crazily off her blue sequined dress when she moved forward into the room.

No less exotic was the woman who stood beside her. Black wavy hair cascaded over one shoulder of a red satin dress set off by a white lacy shawl draped around her arms.

Oozing confidence and walking just slightly behind Danielle was a tall man in his fifties, wearing an open-necked mauve shirt, contrasting brightly with his black suit. Leona walked in behind him.

Kelly's eyes opened wide and he mouth fell open. "Wow! Greg Naples! I never expected to see him in person."

"I loved his last film. He may be getting older, but he's still gorgeous," Laura replied with a sigh.

"Oh my, are we late?" Danielle gracefully waved one arm in a semi-circle and looked helplessly around.

"Not at all," Leona said, stepping up beside her. She faced the room and lightly touched Dani's shoulder. "I'm sure you all know Danielle Davis." She turned and took the man by the arm. "And, of course, Greg Naples really needs no introduction either." Murmurs of agreement came from everyone.

Danielle smiled and nodded. "This is my very good friend, Carmen Rose. You may have heard of her. She's very famous. Well, not as famous as I am." Danielle put her fingers at the base of her neck and giggled.

"Good evening," Carmen said, nodding to the room at large. "Danielle exaggerates. I think it's likely that many of you do not know me."

"Oh. But EVERYONE in OUR circle knows you." Danielle looked around, then apparently decided that this group was not her regular 'circle'. "Perhaps not. Carmen is a psychic and spiritual medium, most appropriate for Halloween, don't you think?" She smiled. "As you know from your invitation, Carmen promised Derek that she would conduct a seance later on. Isn't that fabulous?" She raised her hands and tapped her fingers in mini-applause.

Colonel Montgomery entered the room in time to hear Danielle's last remark. He snorted his contempt. "Nonsensical stuff."

Leona's brow furrowed. "Uncle, I thought you asked Derek specifically to hold a seance tonight."

"I did. Just trying to help Derek spice up the evening a little. Don't believe in that hocus-pocus myself."

Danielle looked offended. Carmen put a restraining hand on her arm. "There are always those who scoff. It does not bother me."

"Dani, perhaps you and Greg would like to come and meet everyone," Leona said in an attempt to thwart an argument from her Uncle.

Always willing to meet her public, Danielle brightened up and started toward Brent's group.

At that moment, Derek came through the door.

"My friends, everyone's here and I'm sure you're all hungry. I've just been informed that dinner's ready. What do you say we adjourn to the dining-room. Cooks don't like to be kept waiting." He smiled. "Right this way." He gestured toward the hallway.

Chapter 3

DINNER

Angie entered first, and pretended to check the place cards. Having made a switch before dinner, she knew exactly where to sit. "Oh. I'm here," she said, in a surprised voice as she took the chair beside Derek.

"How odd," Leona said. "I would have sworn that was Greg's place."

"I guess you were mistaken, Leona. Greg is sitting here," Angie said sweetly, indicating her right side. "There's his card. You must have forgotten."

Leona's face was sour as she took her place on Derek's left and glared across at Angie. *Bitch!*

When everyone was seated, Derek stood up. "I'd like to propose a toast, appropriate to the occasion:

Here's to witches, goblins and ghosts

Who populate Halloween night.

To keep them away from your genial host,

Please try with all your might."

The guests laughed and raised their glasses.

"Why, Derek ... don't tell me you're afraid of witches and ghosts," Brent laughed.

"Maybe he has reason to be," Joe said quietly. Laura poked him in the ribs.

"Sometimes I wonder if there aren't ancestral ghosts lurking about in this place," Derek said. "Check the portraits in the library and see if their eyes don't follow you."

"I can vouch for the fact that they do," Brent said. "Do you remember that night, Derek, when I was visiting and you had that long business call?"

"Sure do. Why don't you tell the story, Brent?"

"Now? I thought the story-telling was scheduled for later on."

"No reason why one can't be told now while we're waiting for the main course. What do you say, folks?" Derek look around the table.

"Go ahead." "Why not?" "Certainly."

"I'm sure we'd all love to hear it," Greg Naples said.

"Just let me finish this ... what is it?" Brent looked at the little menu card. "Eye of newt soup."

"What's a newt?" asked Dani.

"Not-a much. Whatsa newt wit you?" said Joe. Everyone chuckled, except Dani who looked a little puzzled. "Sorry, Dani, I couldn't resist. A newt's a salamander." Joe smiled.

"Sal ... what?"

"Salamander, Dani. Sort of a cross between a frog and a lizard," Greg said

"Ewwwww. And this soup is made from its eye?" Dani looked with horror at her nearly empty bowl.

"No, no, Dani. It's just a name that was used by one of the witches in Macbeth, where they used eye of newt as one of the ingredients to make up a spell-casting potion because a newt contains a mild toxin. They said. I'm not sure if it's true or not, but we just thought it would be a cute name for the soup," Derek explained.

"Oh. Well that's a relief!" Dani pretended great interest in the ceiling, and ignored her soup now left to grow cold in the bowl.

"It is a most excellent soup, no matter what it's name." Greg's spoon clattered against his empty bowl.

Leona smiled. "Thank you, Greg. I'll pass that along to the cook. It's one of her specialties."

Joe glanced at the menu. "Greg, perhaps if you know the whole quote you could recite it now, so that Dani doesn't get too upset when the rest of these delicacies are served."

"Would be my pleasure. Let's see...yes, got it. Dani, this is the verse the second witch used while making their brew:

"Eye of newt, and toe of frog,

Wool of bat, and tongue of dog,

Adder's fork, and blind-worm's sting,

Lizard's leg, and owlet's wing,

For a charm of powerful trouble,

Like a hell broth boil and bubble."

"It all sounds absolutely gross, but I'm sure it will taste good," Dani said, her positive words belied by a phoney smile.

Brent wiped his mouth. "I've finished my newt soup. While we're waiting for the next course - ummm, tongue of dog, I think - I could tell you about the Beckworth ghosts, if you like."

"Great. Go ahead, Brent."

"All right, then." Brent looked round the table and began. "It mostly concerns Derek's grandmother, Sarah. I always think of her as a restless diva."

Chapter 4

RESTLESS DIVA

It was Halloween. I had come over here to talk to Derek and Leona about a fund-raiser that Leona was planning for one of her many charities. We talked for quite a while and after things were pretty much set, Leona retired. Derek and I went into the library for a drink. Derek poured and we started talking about the portraits.

"Didn't anyone ever smile?" I asked.

"I guess they were too busy trying to make money."

"Looks like they were successful," I said, looking from side to side.

"They were. But it costs money to keep up a place like this and it was certainly running out before the diamond strike came in. The money, I mean."

I indicated one of the portraits with my glass. "Is that the grandmother you told me about?"

"That's her. Grandma Sarah Beckworth. She was about thirty-five when that was painted. Quite a gal! She'd sung with the best orchestras in the country, met a lot of people, and attended many parties before she met Grandpa Beckworth. He was a stage door Johnny. She retired from the opera circuit to become mistress of this manor. A prim and proper lady from then on ... most of the time." Derek hesitated. "Used to get Grandpa pissed off when she held her seances. Grandma believed spirits of dead ancestors spoke to her. He used to think she got into the liquor cabinet too often.

We laughed.

Derek pointed to the portrait next to her. "You remember my brother, Colin? Used to work with me some years ago."

"Yes, I remember him. A nice guy. I was sorry to hear of his passing."

"He was her pet. Anything he wanted, he got. Maybe that's the reason we didn't hit it off as brothers. I was the hell-raiser and couldn't bring myself to sit through an opera. Colin, on the other hand, like you, loved the stuff. You would have got along just great with Grandma. You dig the classics."

"Can't deny that," I said. "Colin died in Africa, didn't he?"

"Yes. Made the mistake of trying to break up an argument between two locals. They shoved him away and told him to leave, then ran him off the road as he was heading home. He died in hospital of his injuries without ever regaining consciousness. I had to get a new manager for the mine."

"Very sad."

It was at that moment Derek was informed there was an overseas call for him. He went to his upstairs office to take it. I decided to read while I was waiting and picked out one of the James Patterson books. It seemed I had barely started to read when the rain began. More than just rain. A storm. The thunder was so loud, it shook the fringe of the floor lamp by which I was reading.

A glance through the double glass doors at the fury raging outside made me very happy to be in the comfort of the library. The grandfather clock bonged twelve, the witching hour - the time when ghosts and goblins are supposed to take their best shot at scaring people. I sneered at the idea. Only kids believe in that stuff, right?

I was quite enjoying the novel when an overwhelming smell of lilacs swept over me like a tidal wave. This was followed by a faint, but distinct, rustling sound, like that of a long taffeta dress trailing over a plush carpet. I looked around. No one was there.

The faint strains of an operatic aria began to fill the air, bouncing off the bookcases. I stood up to look for the origin of the music. Nothing. I felt a sudden chill spring up my back and wrap itself around my neck. My breathing quickened as adrenalin began surging. This was something I had never encountered before. I'm usually stoic and unflinching in a crisis. I can handle anything I can see. But this was different.

Reason took over and I thought there had to be a logical explanation. Somewhere. I began to search the room and then the rest of the downstairs. The haunting melody and persistent scent followed me like a bad dream that clings on wakening. Finding nothing, I returned to the library. The storm had abated and I opened the doors and stepped out onto the terrace overlooking the back gardens.

A shadowy male figure appeared suddenly at the bottom of the granite steps. I froze to the spot, my breath trapped somewhere in my throat waiting to be freed. My fingers clutched the cold marble banister as I watched the figure appear to float up the stairs, long, black coat tails fluttering out from behind him.

Straggly gray hair poked out from beneath a tall white hat. Amazingly, none of his clothes were wet. As I peered into the bespectacled face, recognition came with a start. It was Colin, Derek's brother.

I stared in disbelief. "Colin? Colin???"

"Who were you expecting?"

"Uh ... actually no one. What ... I don't understand. You're dead. I think. Aren't you?"

"You're looking at me, aren't you?"

Purely out of reflex, I extended my hand. He clasped mine, but I didn't feel a human hand. All I felt was ... a sensation. Coldness, emptiness.

Colin's eyes took on a glazed look, zombie-like. His speech was hesitant. "I ... lived here ... and we were ... friends." As he spoke, his voice changed in pitch. "I ... need ... you."

That last definitely sounded like a woman. I stood there, mouth agape, not knowing what to say. My voice finally found its way out. "What ... need me for what?"

"I ... can't ... rest. My ... face is ... wet." The high tremolo voice was shrill with intermittent sobs. The shrieking faded away as the figure receded into the darkness.

You can imagine how confused I was. I stood there trying to decide if I had imagined it all. Could I blame James Patterson? There was nothing but blackness beyond the steps. I went back inside.

The book lay waiting, but I couldn't focus on it. Why would Colin come to me? Why did his voice change to that of a woman? What did he - or they - want? And, most pressing of all, was I losing my mind? So many questions. No answers.

Perplexed, I sat in the chair trying to make sense of it all. Was this actually Derek playing some kind of elaborate Halloween prank on me? That seemed like the most obvious and satisfactory answer.

A rumble of approaching thunder cut through my reverie, and I hurried back to the terrace doors. Swift clouds blotted out the pale light of the sickly moon. Periodically, the distant sky lit up as lightning did her dance. Lifted by invisible wings, decayed leaves joined the dance, swirling and twirling as they flew around to the silent tune of the wind. I shut the doors firmly and returned to my chair. A blinding flash of lightning, which momentarily lit the room with 1000 watt voltage, was followed by an ear-splitting crack of thunder that made me jump.

The previously faint sound of the old aria came back, this time louder and more insistent. The cloying smell of lilac perfume became overpowering, reminiscent of a funeral parlour.

Suddenly, the terrace doors flew open allowing a wind-blown wave of rain to splatter my entire head, and a pile of leaves and debris to find a new home on the beige carpet. I jumped to my feet and once again latched the doors.

As I bent to clean up the unwelcome mess, I saw a crumpled sheet of yellowed paper. Very carefully, I unfolded the sodden mass. The edges were elaborately decorated with ornate scrolls. At the top in the middle was a date - October 15, 1920 - and below it, a faded photo of a woman in a long evening gown, a replica of that hanging on the wall. The flyer announced an evening of operatic entertainment, starring Sarah Beckworth in her final appearance.

Something shoved me in the back. I turned quickly. No one was there. I was getting a little tired of this game, if that's what it was. I shouted, "Cut it out, Derek! I know it's you and I've had enough. You can come out now."

Silence. And another push in the back.

"Fine!" I said aloud. "Where do you want me to go?"

The constant pressure directed me out of the library and toward a closet tucked under the staircase in the hallway. I opened the door. Coats of all shapes, sizes and colours hung on ornate, cloth-covered hangers. I chose one that was close to my size.

Boots and shoes were neatly arranged on shelves, except for one boot which was lying on the floor, just below its mate. I picked it up. "Colin" was stencilled on the inside. I couldn't imagine why they would keep boots around that belonged to a dead man. The thought of my brief encounter outside came back, and I realized that nothing that had happened since then made any sense.

Feeling like Alice getting ready to step into the rabbit-hole, I removed my shoes and pulled the boots on; their tightness clamped my feet with a strong grip. They seemed to have a mind of their own and they took me to the umbrella stand not far from the closet, where I retrieved the solitary umbrella and a flashlight which lay on the table next to the container.

It occurred to me that if the invisible 'pusher' was going to send me outside, I had better get a coat from the closet. I found one that was a reasonable fit and followed the inevitable march of my feet back toward the terrace door.

Leaning the umbrella into the wind, I went down the steps. The boots took me past the garden and through a gate onto the dirt path which leads to the family cemetery. With each step I took, the boots squelched and the mud sucked hard, making progress difficult.

I arrived at the cemetery and pushed on the gray metal gate. With squeaks and groans, it finally gave way and I found myself facing five rows of assorted headstones. I had no idea where to go. I needn't have worried.

Under the direction of 'the pusher', I moved cautiously forward, as the flashlight made only a minimal dent in the intense darkness. I went left and then right until I came to a headstone lying face down, barely visible among the soaked leaves which had plastered themselves to the granite. At that moment, 'the pusher' shoved me downward. I understood. I had to set the marker upright.

I leaned the umbrella against a nearby tombstone. Arm muscles complained incessantly as I placed a hand under each side of the stone and heaved it to a standing position. The face was covered with wet mud which I wiped away with the bottom of the coat. There was quite a bit of engraving, and I bent closer to read. "Here lies Sarah Jean Beckworth, Grand Dame of the Opera. Beloved wife of Thomas A. Beckworth. March 5, 1890 - February 12, 1972."

Above the inscription was an oval indent containing an enamelled head and shoulder portrait of Sarah. At last I understood. Sarah didn't like her face being stuck in the wet mud. But why she chose to speak through a man's figure, was still a bafflement.

Very close to Sarah's tombstone was another. I shone the light on it.

"Colin James Beckworth, July 15, 1964 - April 25, 2004."

My feet suddenly felt very cold. I looked down. What fresh hell was this?! The boots were gone! I was going to have to slog back through the mud in my socks, assuming they didn't get swallowed by the mud with the first step. I shivered. The coat had vanished! And the umbrella.

By the time I reached the house, the wind and rain had ceased, and a feeble moon was peeking through the clouds. A blast of very welcome warm air washed over me when I opened the doors. I stepped inside, forgetful of my muddy socks, but their presence, and the damage they were likely doing to the carpet struck me almost immediately. Looking down, I discovered that not only were my socks not muddy, I was wearing perfectly dry clothes and the shoes which I had removed in front of the closet now encased my feet. And there was no sign of the debris which had made itself at home earlier.

It took a minute for my whirling mind to slow down. Had Derek spiked my drink with a hallucinogenic? It didn't seem there could be any other explanation. I must have imagined the whole thing. Except ... I still had the flashlight in my hand.

I hurried to the hall closet. Colin's boots were back where they had been earlier, but now, they were covered in mud. The coat I had worn was wet and muddy at the bottom where I had wiped the face of Sarah Beckworth.

And, yes, the umbrella was back in its home.

Chapter 5

THE WORLD'S HER STAGE

Brent looked around at the other guests. "And that's what happened to me on a Halloween night a few years ago. Now I shall finish my dinner."

Kelly shivered. "Wow! I don't think I'll ever go in that room again."

"What if that tombstone falls over again?" Angie said.

"Not to worry, Angie," Derek said. "After Brent told me his story which, I have to admit I did not at first believe, I had the foundation of the stone replaced. It's quite solid now."

"What convinced you Brent was telling the truth?" said Kelly.

Brent laughed. "Hey! You finally called me Brent."

"It was the stress of the moment," Kelly said, smiling.

"First, I checked the boots and coat, and the next day when the rain had stopped, I took a look at Sarah's tombstone. Needed fixing all right."

"I bet I could play a diva," Dani said.

"Are you an opera singer?" Peter asked.

"Do I have to be?"

"Well, that's what a diva is."

"Really? I thought it meant a royal person, you know, someone with a title like Queen or Duchess. Something like that."

Leona snickered quietly.

"No, my dear. It means a fantastic opera singer," Greg said. "And no doubt you would be wonderful in the role. We can always have someone else dub in the singing."

"Oooh." Dani clapped her hands. "That's a terrific idea. Don't you think so, Derek?"

He glanced at Leona. "Uh, yes. Wonderful."

Leona rolled her eyes and cleared her throat. "As soon as everyone has finished dinner, we'll go back to the living-room."

The conversation dwindled as the guests finished eating.

"Drinks now being served in the drawing-room or you can have more coffee if you wish," Derek said, rising.

Dani rushed to insert herself between Angie and Derek. She took Derek's arm. "I haven't had a chance to talk to you all evening," Dani said in her best, little-girl pouty voice. "I may have a new film coming up soon and we'll need a wonderful producer."

Leona snorted. *Cozy up to him all you want. He's getting no money from me to finance your stupid movies.*

Carmen eyed them and mumbled to herself. "Danger in the air. I sense danger."

Joe glanced at Carmen and frowned. An eyebrow quirked and he moved on.

Angie's eyes narrowed as she watched Dani and Derek leave. She looked around and hurried to catch up to Peter. "Peter, you must come with me and tell me all about yourself," she said, pushing Kelly aside and grabbing his arm. Angie ushered him into a loveseat near the fireplace. Looking somewhat taken aback, Kelly seated herself in the chair on Peter's left.

Derek remained standing after everyone had settled down. "Ladies and gentlemen. I hope you all enjoyed your special Halloween dinner."

"Spectacular, darling." Danielle jumped up and pressed herself against Derek. "Worthy of an article in Food Today, wouldn't you agree?" Dani clapped her hands and looked around in encouragement. "Applause! Applause!"

Enthusiastic applause followed, along with congratulatory remarks.

"Look at her! Always wants to be the centre of attention," Angie hissed in Peter's ear.

He looked at Angie's eyes. *If looks could kill.* "Do you know her well?"

"Enough to know that she's got her hooks out for Derek. She'd better be careful."

Peter looked quizzically at Angie, who was glaring in Danielle's direction. "What ... " His question was interrupted by their host.

"Thank you, my friends. There's a bar set up in the den behind me in case the waiter doesn't have what you want on his tray. If everyone has a drink, I think it's time to get on with the highlight of the evening ... your scary stories."

The anticipation and excitement on several of the faces was not diffused by groans from a few of the guests.

"Of course, we have to have the right atmosphere," Derek continued, putting his hand on the wall switches. Immediately, the lamps all went out, leaving the now-dying fire as the only light in the room. The ceiling turned into a dark, night sky, its centre illuminated by a large harvest moon. The ghosts now truly appeared to fly in luminescent splendor.

"Ooooh. How lovely!" Danielle raised her arms to the ceiling.

"Just one more thing to set the scene." Derek pulled a tall stool close to the doorway of the den and pressed another switch. A soft blue spotlight came to life, centred on the stool. "Now that the scene is set ... who would like to start?"

Silence.

"Come now, don't be shy. Danielle, why don't you lead us off?"

"Well, if you insist, darling." Danielle perched on the stool provided for the storyteller. The slit in her dress opened, revealing a long, curvy leg, eerily glowing blue from the spotlight.

"Going to be hard to concentrate on the story looking at that," Joe Walters hissed in Brent's ear.

Brent nodded.

"My grandmother told me this story when I was a little girl. It isn't really scary, exactly, but I always thought it was very romantic and would make a good movie, with me playing the role of Juliet, of course. I can do English accents quite well." Danielle smiled. "We called it 'The Necklace.'" Danielle looked around to make sure all eyes were on her. Satisfied, she began.

Chapter 6

THE NECKLACE

It was the most magnificent necklace Juliet had ever seen. As Madame Fitzhugh turned her head to inspect her hairdo, Juliet watched the shafts of light shoot from the leaf-shaped emeralds which pointed the way to the huge ruby rose, surrounded by diamonds, that was nearly blinding in its brilliance.

"Hmmm. I guess that will have to do. I wish you knew how to make a French roll. A French roll would make me look younger."

The fact that her hair was too sparse to be rolled seemed to escape Marguerite Fitzhugh, and no hairdo would remove the frown lines accumulated over sixty years of nearsightedness. She continued, "I see you are admiring my necklace. It is rather nice, isn't it? Captain Fitzhugh brought it from India for me."

The necklace had been the talk of the household since Hubert Fitzhugh's return. Alice, the parlourmaid who had been serving tea when Marguerite opened the velvet case, wasted no time in delivering tales of the beauty of the necklace to the servants gathered around the kitchen supper table, but this was Juliet's first look at it.

"Indeed, ma'am. It is breathtaking. I've never seen anything like it."

"I daresay you haven't, given your background. I'm sure that parsonage coffers aren't exactly overflowing with gold." Marguerite's lip curled in distaste.

Juliet smiled inwardly as she thought of what the old cow would say if she knew the truth. Aloud, she said, "Quite right, Madame."

"It's time for me to make my entrance. Hand me that fan. I'm to be seated next to Signor Gianelli and his breath always smells disgusting."

Sounds of music and laughter floated up the stairs as Juliet opened the door.

"See that you are awake when the party is over. I shall need help with my clothes." Marguerite sailed through the door in waves of dusting powder and eau de cologne.

"Yes, madame." Juliet leaned against the closed door and smiled. "You better believe I'll be awake." The clock on the chimneypiece chimed seven times. Only two hours till Bert's arrival.

Just before nine, Juliet made her way between the scuttling maids and cooks who were serving a variety of desserts to the hundred or so guests.

Unnoticed in the whirlwind of activity, she pocketed a couple of bannock buns in case Bert happened to be hungry, and darted quickly through the back entrance. She shivered in the coolness of the April night and drew her shawl closer around her shoulders. An owl hooted in the distance. Suddenly, a hand covered her mouth.

"Shhhh. It's me, love." Bert swiftly removed his hand and replaced it with his lips.

Juliet drew back from the kiss and looked into Bert's brown eyes, darker now in the light of the moon. She pinched his cheek. "You scared me half to death."

He held her tight. "Sorry, love. I was afraid you might let out a scream if I startled you by speaking."

"Rather give me a heart attack instead, would you?" she said, laughing.

"How's it going inside?" Bert nodded toward the house. " Sounds like a royal rumble."

"I stayed well away from everyone, just in case one of my previous employers was invited."

"Good girl."

Juliet put her face close to Bert's, not too difficult as they were almost the same height. Her eyes opened wide and eyebrows shot up. "But, Bert...most wonderful news. Just like I hoped, the old cow got that fabulous necklace out of the bank and she's wearing it tonight. Must be worth a fortune. We'll be able to add that to the rest. We've hit the jackpot this time, love."

Bert smiled and waved his fists by his head. "Fantastic!"

"Have you got the tickets?"

Bert patted the top right of his jacket. "Right here. Our passage is booked and we sail tomorrow from Southampton. And now that everything's set, we've got some spare time. I've missed you." Bert's arms encircled Juliet and he kissed her passionately.

"Not here, Bert. There's a quiet spot in the stable."

"Won't be quiet for long, I'm thinking." Bert laughed as the two hurried through the night.

The sound of voices and clopping of horses' hooves made them aware that several hours had passed. They kissed goodbye and Bert slipped into the darkness as Juliet hurriedly pulled on her clothes and scampered back to the house. She stood in the upper hall, getting her breath back before going into the bedroom to turn down the bed. She ignited the logs in the fireplace and returned to the hall. Leaning over the upper railing, Juliet watched Marguerite Fitzhugh approach the stairs.

"Hubert, if you ever invite that Signor Gianelli again, I refuse to have him sit beside me, no matter how much his friendship means to you. I have a splitting headache from trying to understand what he was saying, not to mention an upset stomach from breathing the same air. I'm going to bed now and don't want to be disturbed until very late tomorrow morning."

Hubert looked up at his wife. "As you wish, my dear. Would you like a glass of brandy to help get rid of your headache? I'm taking one up with me."

"No thank you. I shall take a dose of laudanum ... for curative purposes."

"Very well, dear. Till morning." He headed to his study.

Juliet smiled. Curative purposes, indeed. The old gal was addicted to it and, unknown to her husband, took it every night. Juliet drew back as Marguerite began to climb the stairs.

Once in bed, Marguerite demanded the laudanum. Juliet obliged, adding a little extra to the glass. Marguerite swallowed the dose and sank back onto her pillows with a sigh.

Juliet spent longer than usual fussing over Marguerite's clothes, waiting for the laudanum to take effect. She fiddled with the drapes and bedcovers until Marguerite's breathing deepened.

"Oh, Madame, you have forgotten to put away your necklace. What a pity that you have to get out of bed again." This was the moment on which the entire plan hinged. Juliet held her breath.

Marguerite groaned, half-sat, then sank back again. "I am not getting out of this bed. You put it away in the safe."

"I do not know where the key is, Madame," Juliet lied.

"Oh bother. Bring me that Chinese puzzle box." As Juliet watched, Marguerite pushed a few tiles and a secret compartment opened up. She handed the key to Juliet. "Here. When you're done, just put the key back and push a few of those squares." Marguerite flopped back on her pillows.

"Very well, Madame." Juliet turned away, removed a pouch from her pocket and slipped the necklace inside. She opened the safe and quickly added the rest of the jewellery to the pouch. "All done, Madame."

Without opening her eyes, Marguerite mumbled something.

"Good-night, Madame." Juliet extinguished the lamp and quietly left the room. She retraced her steps to the stable where Bert waited with their horses.

"Did you get it?" he asked.

"All of it. Let's go. We've just got time to catch the train."

Too excited to sleep, Juliet thought of the new country which, in just a few days, they would be calling home, and most of all, of the beautiful jewellery that would guarantee them a wonderful life. *Maybe we will have enough money from the other stuff so I can keep the necklace for myself.*

The train was half an hour late arriving in Southampton, but that still left plenty of time for them to get something to eat and head for the docks. Just before noon, Juliet and Bert made their way through the crowd of onlookers and climbed aboard the huge ocean liner. They stood at the rail and waved to the watching strangers.

Juliet linked her arm in Bert's and leaned against him. "Bert, do you think I might keep that ruby necklace? It is such a beauty. We could sell everything else, but maybe not that. I would love to wear it some day with an elegant gown. What do you say?"

Bert smiled at her. "Let's see how it goes when we get to America, love. We've got a whole lifetime to plan." He pulled Juliet tighter against his body.

Two blasts from the ship's funnels rent the air. The lines were cast off. RMS Titanic was underway.

Chapter 7

THE CON GAME

Danielle sighed. "Grandmom told me they drowned like so many of the third class passengers. Such a sad ending." She looked expectantly around at the gathering.

"Very nice presentation, Danielle," Derek said, clapping. The others joined in.

"Thank you," Danielle said. "But if they ever make it into a movie, I'd like to have it end with me and my lover escaping the disaster and becoming con artists in the U. S." Danielle giggled. "I've always wanted to play a con artist."

"It seems to me she'd be better suited as the other woman," Leona said, looking pointedly at her husband.

Derek drew a deep breath. "For God's sake, Leona. Don't be ridiculous!" He turned back to the guests.

"Does she not know they made a Titanic move - movie with DiCaprio and whatshername?" Angie said, leaning hard into Peter's shoulder.

"Probably figures hers would be better," he replied, pulling back from her boozy breath.

Kelly turned and touched Peter's arm. "I love con artist movies."

Before Peter had a chance to reply, Joe Walters piped up. "Cons aren't good if you're the victim."

"True, of course. But we're talking about movies, where the con guys are usually rather lovable characters," said Peter.

"Quite often the real ones are lovable too. That's how they get away with their scams in the first place. By the time the victim realizes they've been taken, 'Mr. Lovable' has disappeared," Joe said.

"There certainly have been a lot of good-looking serial killers, that's for sure." Kelly shuddered.

"For sure. You just never know." Peter nodded.

"You can't live your life in fear, though. That wouldn't be living at all," Kelly said. "Still, it's scary to be dating these days because you just never know what the person is truly like. They may appear friendly and kind and quite normal until you're alone with them. Or married. Even some wives have been fooled. Such a sweet guy at home, and off killing people at night." Kelly hugged herself.

"That's true. Some of them travel around the country, but many of them stay in one place and commit their crimes elsewhere. They could be anyone," Peter nodded. "Could be the guy next door."

"That reminds me." Joe stood up. "Brent, I'll tell the next tale, if you like."

"Of course, Joe. Come on up."

Joe seated himself. "This is a little different from the last one. Hope you like it. I heard it a long time ago and in my mind, I always called it 'The Hunger.'"

Chapter 8

THE HUNGER

Gerry Davis was getting more irritable by the minute. It had been a long drive, and even longer since she had last eaten. Her mood darker than the impending nightfall, Gerry pressed harder on the gas pedal. Rounding a sharp bend in the road, she was greeted by a flashing neon sign obscenely glowing blood red against the blackening sky. "Tex's Roadhouse" it proudly proclaimed and under that " otel Vacan y".

"Yay, Tex, whoever you are. I thank you for building a motel in the boonies."

To her surprise, there were several trucks and a couple of beat-up cars in the parking lot in front of the main building. Honky-tonk music blared out through a wooden screen door, leaving no doubt as to the location of the roadhouse side of the business. A hand-lettered sign in the cracked pane of a second door on the far left side of the building, indicated the office of the 'otel' part of the establishment.

Gerry pulled her van alongside a truck, through the back window of which she could see a rifle sling, fully occupied. "Good ol' boys," she thought, grabbing her purse and heading for the door. A thump of her hip was necessary to force the recalcitrant door to give way. "Figures," she mumbled.

"Be right there," an invisible female voice called. Gerry looked at the dismal room, featuring wallpaper that Jesse James might have viewed as a young man.

"Sorry to keep you waiting." The woman ran her rough hands over her bottle blonde hair. "My name's Peggy. Ya need a room?" Gerry noticed the woman's eyes glance appraisingly over her navy slacks and jacket.

"Yes, please. Just for tonight. I was really surprised to find a motel way out here."

"Yeah, I know we're a bit out of the way now. Used to be a highway, but it got moved." Peggy opened a large book and turned it toward Gerry. "You travelin' alone?"

"Yes, there's just me." Gerry signed where Peggy's finger indicated.

"You're pretty brave. I'd be scared to travel by myself. Petey - my husband always goes with me."

"Oh."

"How're you paying for this? We don't have one of them bank thingies, but I can write up a credit card charge."

"Credit card is fine." Gerry handed over her plastic and studied the woman as she pulled out the credit card machine. Thin, foxy face with hollow cheeks and a hardness bespoke of someone who had seen it all, Peggy could have been any age from twenty to forty-five.

Peggy passed the completed form for Gerry's signature, her eyes focussing on the sparkle of Gerry's diamond rings. "Gettin' away from your husband for a while, Mrs. Davis?" The woman sighed. "Sure wouldn't mind gettin' away from mine for a bit." A wistful smile made her face almost pretty.

"I travel for my job. My husband was killed in a car accident a year ago."

"Oh, I'm sorry. I didn't mean nuthin'."

"I know you didn't. Maybe you should learn to drive - make yourself more independent." Gerry smiled. "Can I get something to eat next door?"

"Oh sure. Billy makes real good wings and ribs. Tell him you're stayin' here and he'll give you a special deal. You can charge it to your room, too," Peggy added proudly. "Here's your key. You're in room 6. If there's anything you need, just holler. You'll have to come by the office though cause we don't have no phone in the room."

"Oh. Okay, thanks."

"No problem. Have a good night."

A single light bulb did little to illuminate the area in front of the cabins which comprised the 'otel'. Even the car's bright headlights had difficulty picking up the '6' tacked onto the door. Retrieving her luggage and sample case, Gerry pulled in a small breath of the damp night air and opened the door to the cabin.

She ran her fingers over the wall to the right until she located a light switch that turned on a lamp by the bed. To her surprise and relief, the room was quite clean, although the furniture was obviously old. Gerry sat on the bed. The room reminded her of the first motel where she and Charlie had made love. That was long before they were married and Charlie had made money on the stock market.

Gerry sighed. She missed him so much, especially during the lonely nights where self pleasure seemed like such a poor substitute. Sex with Charlie had been fabulous. Erotic thoughts of his fingers tracing a line down between her breasts, moving slowly downwards, made her ache inside. Unconsciously, her hand moved to her crotch. She closed her eyes and drew a deep breath.

She thought about her life since leaving the clinic. Traveling around the country didn't leave much room for establishing a relationship even if she had wanted to. Not that she hadn't had offers, but somehow having sex with someone else seemed disloyal to Charlie. She could almost hear Dr. Cameron telling her that was a silly notion. Charlie was dead. Well, maybe to the rest of the world, but to her, he still seemed pretty much alive.

Sometimes she thought she saw him just watching her. It seems men didn't care if she'd had a nervous breakdown or not. Especially Mark. He had made it pretty plain that he would love to take her out. No doubt he would have wanted to end the evening in bed.

Thinking of her boss brought Gerry back to reality. She decided she'd better check the address of McKenzie Pharmacy. From her sample case, she retrieved the sales sheet and Yahoo map printout. Apparently, somewhere along the way, she had made a wrong turn. The only good news was that the road outside the motel eventually would rejoin the main highway, according to the map.

In spite of her insistent stomach, Gerry decided to unpack and change her clothes. She threw a nightgown and bathrobe over the back of a chair. She was happy to find the bathroom clean and serviceable, despite the odd chip in the floor and wall tiles. Gerry set her sample case on the counter, opened it up and removed the toiletries she carried in there for convenience. She refreshed her makeup and went back to the bedroom.

After changing into the pale yellow sweater which everyone told her complemented her chestnut hair, she pulled on a pair of jeans. Deciding to take Peggy's suggestion of charging her meals to the room, Gerry put her purse into the night table drawer beside the Gideon Bible. *Take care of my purse.* She smiled at the thought.

Gerry walked back around the building and headed for the screen door. A beery blast of smoke and heat accompanied the still-playing honky-tonk music. Several men and women occupying the bar stools stared at her when she walked in; people at the tables were too busy with their food to pay much attention.

"Sit anywhere you want, miss," the bartender called. "Alice'll be right out."

Out of the corner of her eye, Gerry was vaguely aware of a man standing in the shadows of the washroom hallway.

She placed her order with the buxom Alice, lit a cigarette retrieved from the pack in her pocket, and leaned back to people watch. In time with the music, a young couple were rubbing against each other in a slow, sexual mating dance. Knowing where they would end up created a different hunger deep within Gerry's loins.

"Look like they're having fun, don't they miss?"

Gerry turned and found herself looking up at a tall, thirty-something male dressed in tight jeans and a blue flannel shirt, open at the neck. Smoky blue-gray eyes seemed to pierce right through her sweater, his overt sexiness dangerous in its intensity.

"Care to join them while you're waiting for your food?" Smiling, he reached out and put his hand under her elbow.

"I...uh...I'm not sure ..."

"Come on, it'll help pass the time. My name's Jim."

His touch sent a charge through her. Gerry rose and moved the short distance to the dance floor. Jim's muscular arms drew her close and she could feel the strength of his chest pressing against hers. The heat from their bodies fuelled the fire within, and much as she tried to turn it off, Gerry's desire grew. It had been so terribly long since anyone had held her like this. So long since ...

"What's your name, darlin'?"

"Gerry," she said. Her voice croaked, constricted by the raging feelings within.

"Haven't seen you in here before. I sure would have noticed a beautiful woman like you." Gerry could feel his hot breath as Jim spoke close to her ear.

Gerry's emotions were in turmoil. She was torn between running away and staying in his arms, but all thinking gave way to the excitement which coursed through her body. Turning her head and leaning back slightly, her lips came temptingly close to his.

He looked straight into her eyes, not sure if he was reading her correctly. Satisfied at what he saw, his hand slid down over her buttocks and pressed her body tightly against his maleness.

"Are you staying here, Gerry?"

"Yes," she whispered, throwing caution to the wind.

"Great. Maybe ...looks like your food's just arriving," he said, dropping his arms.

Gerry reluctantly stepped away and they made their way back to the table.

"Alice, honey, bring me a red wine, would ya?"

Alice smiled knowingly at Jim and cast a glance at Gerry. "Sure. Comin' right up."

"Are you not having something to eat?" Gerry asked.

"I already ate, darlin'. In fact, I was just about ready to leave when I saw you come in. I said to myself, now there's a real woman, and one I definitely want to meet."

Gerry flushed. "You're embarrassing me."

"Nothing to be embarrassed about. You're much too beautiful to be sitting alone. The way I figure is you had a fight with your husband or boyfriend and just wanted to keep away for a while. Am I right?"

She shook her head. "Actually no. I don't have a husband or a boyfriend."

He picked up her hand. "I find that hard to believe, especially with them big diamonds on your left hand." He tapped the ring.

"Oh. Well, I was married, but ..." Gerry hesitated. She didn't pull her hand away.

"He was mean to you and you got a divorce." Jim raised her hand to his lips and then caressed his cheek with it.

"No, no. Not at all. He was killed in a car accident."

Jim enclosed her hand in both of his. "I'm sorry, darlin'. How did it happen?" He pulled his chair close to her.

Gerry squirmed in her seat. Talking about it would bring back the awful memories.

Jim saw her reluctance. He rubbed her hand on his cheek then kissed it again. "You don't have to tell me if you don't want to. I don't mean to pry."

Gerry was confused. He was just being kind. "It ... I was driving. A transport came out of a side road. I swerved to avoid it, hit a guardrail. Charlie's side of the car bounced into the back end of the transport. He hit his head on the window and died before the ambulance came. I don't remember much except for the blood. Charlie's blood. It was all over me." Tears were close to the surface as she remembered the horror of that night.

Jim put his arm around her and pulled her head to his shoulder. "I'm so sorry, darlin'. I should never have asked you about it." He pushed her long hair out of her face.

Gerry sniffled. "No, no. It's all right. Dr. Cameron says I should be able to talk about it as part of the healing process."

"Who's Dr. Cameron?"

She lifted her head and dabbed her eyes with the cocktail napkin. "My psychiatrist. I had a nervous breakdown after the accident and they kept me in hospital for three months. I still visit him once a month."

"Well, I just feel like some big dumb jackass of a fool." He rubbed his hand through his hair. "Here I thought we were going to have a pleasant evening together and I've gone and got you all upset. Drink up your wine and I'll get you another. It'll do you some good." Jim signalled to the bartender.

"Oh no. You didn't upset me, you were just being interested and kind." Gerry finished her wine just as the next glass arrived.

"I hope you haven't lost your appetite for your dinner. Billy makes damn fine ribs."

Gerry looked at her plate and wished she had ordered something less messy than ribs and wings. She didn't examine the reason why that thought popped into her head.

"Maybe you don't eat much anyway. That's how you keep that great figure," Jim said, watching her pick through her food. "Not too hungry?" He chuckled. "For food anyway. Bet you have an appetite for something else though."

Gerry blushed. It was as if he were reading her mind. "I think I've had enough," Gerry said. "But I'll finish the wine."

"So what brings you to this neck of the woods?" Jim asked.

"I'm hired by a drug company to travel around to different pharmacies, picking up outdated medicines and things that have been returned to them. Usually, I don't get lost like I did today."

"Well, I must say I'm rather happy you got lost. Gave me the chance to meet you," Jim smiled and leaned in closer, "and hopefully get to know you a whole lot better." He put his hand tenderly on the side of her face.

Gerry's heart quickened. She set the empty glass down.

"Do you want some more wine?" Jim said.

"Oh no. No thanks. I think I've had enough for now."

Jim leaned closer and took her hand. His warm breath caressed her cheek. "Did you wanna dance some more or should we go someplace quieter to ... talk?"

Waves of pheromones washed over her, leaving no doubt of what he had in mind. Gerry swallowed hard. Her heart was thumping loudly. "I guess we could go to my room," she said.

Jim left some money on the table to pay for their orders. He put his arm around her as they headed towards the door. Once outside, Jim embraced her, kissing her passionately. When he drew back, she was breathless.

"Just a second, darlin'. I've got to get something out of my truck." He leaned in and brought out two bottles of wine, one red and one white. "Always be prepared, I say. Just like a Boy Scout."

Arms encircling each other, they hurried to her room. Gerry switched on the light and Jim placed the bottles on the dresser.

He came over to her. "Turn the light off, honey. There might be nosey neighbours."

As far as she knew, there were no other occupants in the 'otel', but she was beyond drawing any sensible conclusions.

Jim pulled the sweater over her head and undid her bra. He leaned down and kissed her breasts. Gerry moaned. He undressed quickly, as she let her jeans and panties slip to the floor.

"God, you're beautiful," Jim said. He pulled her to him, forced her mouth open with his tongue and kissed her passionately as his hands worked magic around her body. Without letting her lips leave his, Jim picked her up and laid her on the bed.

The hunger within Gerry exploded as Jim began kissing and sucking on her nipples. She ran her hands over his arms and across his back, pulling him as close as possible. His lips travelled down her body, heightening her arousal. When his tongue and fingers touched her most private spot, an electric jolt shot through her body and her body arched. All Gerry's long-repressed passion burst forth in a frenzy as he finally entered her.

Satiated at last, he moved off her, and she lay there gasping, wishing he had stayed with her instead of rolling away.

"Are you all right, darlin'?" he called over his shoulder.

"Fine."

Jim flipped on the night table lamp. "How about some wine?" he said, getting up.

Still trembling, Gerry watched his naked athletic body cross to the dresser. She felt deserted somehow and weak, and wondered how he was able to jump out of bed so quickly. Jim grabbed the cups by the coffee machine, filled them and handed her one. "Well, they ain't fancy, but they'll hold the drink."

Gerry slowly sat up, and swung her legs over the side of the bed. She took the cup and sipped the wine while Jim swallowed half a cup.

"You got pretty worked up there." He smiled. "Sure easy to turn you on. Must've been a long time."

Gerry stared at him and her arm slowly lowered the cup.

He retrieved a pack of cigarettes from his shirt pocket and threw it back on the floor. Jim looked at her and smiled. "You're the best piece of tail I've had in a long time, baby. Smoke?" He held out the package.

Gerry was taken aback and suddenly became conscious of her nakedness. Hurriedly, she got up, dropped the cup on the night table and grabbed her bathrobe off the back of the chair.

"What's the matter, Gerry? Shy?" Jim laughed. "Don't worry. I've seen plenty of naked women before. Of course, they didn't all have great tits like yours."

Gerry was horrified and hurt by Jim's casual attitude. Guilt overwhelmed her. *What have I done? What will Charlie think of me?* "I ... you... You've done this with lots of other women?"

Jim laughed. "Hey, come on. Surely you didn't think you were something special? It's only sex. People do it everyday." Jim lay back on the bed, put the cigarette in his mouth and waggled his penis. "Give me half an hour and I'll be good to go again. Betcha'd like that babe." He took a long drag and blew the smoke out in a perfect circle.

Gerry hurried into the bathroom and leaned over the sink. She felt dirty, used. *What in God's name was I thinking? Some stranger comes on to me, gives me wine and I jump into bed with him!*

She thought she was going to throw up and clutched her stomach. The nausea passed and Gerry looked at herself in the mirror. Over her shoulder she saw Charlie staring reproachfully at her. She splashed cold water on her face. Charlie was still watching. Was that a tear on his face?

"I'm sorry, Charlie. I just miss you so much." She put her hand on the glass. *"You know I still love you. I will always love you. Please forgive me. Please. I'm begging you."* The face with

the sorrowful eyes faded away. She was crying now. *How could I have done this when dear Charlie is waiting at home for me? I'm so mixed up. What can I do? Poor, sweet Charlie. He'll never forgive me for this and who could blame him. But wait. Maybe he doesn't know yet. His tears might have been because he missed me too. He must never know. It will be my deep, dark secret.*

But what if this Jim guy called me or emailed, or worse, called Charlie directly? Her mind flew in several directions. *He must be stopped. Charlie must not be told. It is up to me to make sure that he never knows. But how?*

Her eyes came to rest on the skull and crossbones on one of the vials picked up from her last stop. They told her what to do. Gerry picked up a syringe and inserted it into the vial. She entered the bedroom.

"There you are. I was beginning to think you weren't coming back, darlin'. Come on over here. Big Daddy's got another present for you," he said, pointing to his growing erection.

Gerry forced a smile. "That's nice. But I'd like a drink first. Let me refill yours."

"Well, thanks, sweetheart. I never turn down a drink."

"I'd like a smoke now, too, Jim. Light it for me?"

"Sure. Whatever you want." Jim leaned to the other side of the bed to retrieve the pack from his shirt.

Gerry swiftly shot the contents of the syringe into his wine and slipped the needle behind the coffee pot.

"Here you are, Jim," Gerry said, handing him the wine and taking the cigarette.

"Thanks, babe."

"How about a contest?" she said, "to see which wine bottle will be empty first." Gerry nodded toward the wine bottles. "Red, you win, white I win."

"And what do I get if I win?" Jim leered at her.

"You get to spend the rest of the night with me."

He laughed and stood up. "I'll drink to that," he said and tossed back the contents of the cup without hesitation. "That tasted kind of ..."

The cup dropped to the floor as Jim clutched his throat. He gasped for air. "Can't ... breathe." He fell to the floor. In moments, his jerky movements stopped.

Gerry looked down at him and then over at Charlie standing near the door. "He deserved it, Charlie," she said, turning her head and waving her arm toward the body. "I didn't mean to do anything wrong. He made me do it. I just miss you so." She clasped her hands. "Please don't hate me."

Gerry stepped over Jim's body. "Come and lie down with me, Charlie," she said, climbing into the bed. She looked at the door. Charlie had disappeared. Gerry jumped out of bed and ran to the door. "Charlie! Come back!" He was nowhere in sight.

Sobbing, she returned to the bed, buried her head in a pillow and cried until sleep overtook her.

Jim spent the night with her, but not in the way he had anticipated.

Chapter 9

AND THEN

Joe looked around at several shocked faces. “Surprised?” he asked.

“Oh my God! That poor woman. Is it true?” Kelly said.

“Sure surprised me.” Brent shook his head. “I thought they were just going to have a little fling and she’d be cured. So was she a serial killer?”

“Of course not. Women aren’t serial killers.” Leona looked offended.

Colonel Montgomery cleared his throat. “Actually, there are many cases of women serial killers. What about Lizzie Borden?”

“Who?” said Kelly.

“Long before your time, my dear. Long before. I’ll be happy to tell you about it.” The Colonel started to rise.

"Oh, um, thank you for the offer, Thomas, but perhaps some other time? There are other stories to be told here tonight," Derek said quickly.

The Colonel sat back and Kelly sighed in relief.

Peter Morrison chuckled. "Quick thinking."

"I think it's disgusting. I certainly wouldn't want to play the part of a female serial killer," Danielle said, screwing up her face.

Carmen patted Danielle's hand. "You are much too beautiful to be a serial killer, Danielle."

Angie spoke up. "But you would make a wonderful ... what do they call the female equivalent of a lady killer? A man-killer?"

"These days, if she's an older woman who goes after a younger man, she's called a cougar," Leona said, looking pointedly at Angie, now snuggled up to Peter Morrison.

Angie gave her a frozen stare and tossed down the rest of her drink. "Bitch," she said, under her breath. "She's at least five years older than I am."

Kelly leaned forward in her chair. "Joe, you never answered me. Is that a true story?"

Joe nodded his head. "Sadly, it is, Kelly. Happened out in the Midwest."

"Well what became of her?" Leona said, flinging out her hands. "They must have found the body."

"Oh yes. When she didn't check out of the room, Peggy came around to see if she wanted to stay longer. Gerry was just sitting in a chair staring into space, and Jim was where he'd fallen. The police were called, of course, but there was never a trial because Gerry was considered to be unfit. They sent her back to the sanatorium to be under the care of Dr. Cameron again. She was there for five years before being deemed to be cured." He paused. "They were wrong."

"What??" Leona and Kelly said in the same breath.

Joe's smile was grim. "They were wrong. About six months after her release, the police were baffled by a series of killings. The men were last seen in the company of a woman, and were all found dead the next morning from cyanide poisoning."

"Lord," said Greg, "that's enough to make you celibate - or gay."

Leona gave a start as if an idea had just crossed her mind.

"The pattern in all the cases was the same, but the descriptions of the woman were different. - blonde, brunette, redhead, glasses, no glasses."

Leona tipped her head sideways. "Are you a policeman, Joe?"

Joe smiled. "You found me out." He chuckled. Not any more. Used to be. Now I work in the private sector."

"Private investigator?" Leona asked, eyes wide.

Joe nodded. "Yes."

Greg leaned forward, left elbow on knee, chin supported by his hand. "So was the woman ever caught?"

Joe drew in a deep breath and faced Greg. "Yes. It took them two years to catch up with her."

"They should have asked me. I would have found her sooner," Carmen said.

"Oooh, I'm sure you would. Carmen is a wonderful psychic," Danielle said, her hand fluttered toward Carmen.. "She told me that I would be getting a new part soon, and I'm just waiting to hear from my agent. And maybe I can convince Derek to be the producer." She raised her eyebrows, tipped her head sideways and looked at Derek, a coy smile on her lips.

"Balderdash!" Colonel Montgomery thundered and pointed with his pipe at Carmen. "Psychics are nothing but hokum."

Derek frowned. "Wait a minute, Thomas. I thought you asked me to have Carmen conduct a seance."

The Colonel's mouth fell slightly open and he figuratively retreated. "Er, um, I did. Like I told Leona, I was just trying to spice up your evening."

"The truth is, you were hoping to prove that I was a phoney."

He nodded his head. "Madame ... you are correct. At least partly."

Carmen drew herself up. "Sir, not all psychics are phoney. Some are very honest. Police departments have used us to search for missing people, and it's a fact that I, personally, helped the Memphis P.D. find the body of a missing child."

"Did you? That's most interesting," said Peter Morrison. "Maybe I should have hired you to find my father."

"What happened to your father, Peter?" said Kelly.

Peter shrugged his shoulders and threw up his hands. "He simply disappeared."

"Maybe he ran off with another woman," said Angie. She raised an eyebrow and looked pointedly at Leona.

"Never happen. Dad wasn't that kind of man," Peter retorted, pulling away from Angie.

"All men are 'that kind of man' as far as I'm concerned," Leona piped up, looking at her husband. "Of course, it's not always a woman they run off with. Don't you agree, Derek?"

Derek looked puzzled. "What?"

"What I think is that if a couple is happily married, the man won't go looking elsewhere," said Laura. "What do you think, Mr. Richardson?"

"I'm inclined to agree with you, Laura, but I'm not a psychologist and who knows why anyone does what they do."

"I, of course, quite often know what people have in their minds," said Carmen.

"Are you saying you're a mind reader?" asked Kelly.

"I can be blocked, of course, but - certainly. For instance, I know right now that the young man sitting near you is very interested in dating you and you feel the same way."

Kelly blushed.

"You hardly need to be a mind reader to know when people are interested in each other," said Leona. "It's usually pretty obvious. Wouldn't you agree, Angie?"

"Well ..."

"Of course, that interest might be misplaced, especially if one of them doesn't know what the other person is really like. We all have secrets, don't we Derek?" Leona asked , honey dripping from her tone.

"I'm not sure I know what you're talking about," Derek said through clenched teeth.

"Never mind. Doesn't matter. Time will tell." Leona looked around at the guests. "Talking about men who fool around," her eyes travelled to Derek, "reminds me of a story I heard a while back from a local when I was visiting the midwest. I'll go next."

Chapter 10

RAY

Peaceful Valley was anything but peaceful in the Prentice household. Walls shook, furniture was knocked over and floors vibrated under the impact of heavy boots on a daily basis. One of the inhabitants lived in fear.

Ray Prentice shoved his wife in the back, nearly knocking her out of bed. "Get up, you lazy bitch. I want a decent breakfast before going to work."

Kate caught herself on the night table and staggered to her feet. Tears filled her eyes as she headed for the kitchen. With shaking hands she filled the coffee maker and decided she'd better make pancakes, Ray's favourite, to go with the bacon and eggs. Delicious breakfast smells soon filled the room.

Ray clomped in and sat down at the table. Kate immediately hurried over to tie up his logging boots. Ray slurped his coffee, looked at the heaping plate of food and stuck his fork in a pancake. "These pancakes ain't cooked enough," he said, slamming his fork down on the table.

"I've got more here." Kate brought over another plate. Ray grunted and stuffed a slice of bacon in his mouth.

"Why're you standing there like some kind of idiot? Sit down and drink a coffee with me."

Kate took a seat opposite Ray. "Are you coming home tonight?" she asked.

Sometimes he stayed away for a week if he didn't feel like driving the forty-odd miles home, or if Patsy Morgan's husband was out-of-town on business.

Ray stared at her, a sly look in his eyes. Kate wished she hadn't said anything. "Why? You plannin' on goin' somewheres if I don't?"

"No, no. Of course not. You know I don't go nowhere without you, Ray."

He shoved another big forkful of food in his mouth. "Then why you askin' if I'm comin' home?"

"We're gonna need some milk, that's all. I just thought..."

Ray snorted. "You thought. There's a laugh."

"I mean we need milk. Maybe you could pick it up on your way home."

"Why didn't you get enough when we went to the store last time?" Ray waved his fork at her. "Just like you. Don't think ahead. Stupid."

"That was a week ago. We're just about out."

"We'll see." Ray shoved his plate away. "Can't eat no more of that shit." He wiped his mouth on his sleeve. "C'mere," he said, standing up.

Ray pulled Kate to him, pinched her breast and kissed her hard on the mouth. "Don't let nobody in while I'm gone. There's lots of bad people out there." Spittle mixed with a bit of food landed on Kate's chin.

"I won't, Ray."

"If you do, there'll be trouble," he said, squeezing her shoulders.

She tried not to flinch from the pain. "I won't let nobody in, Ray."

He pushed her away and she quickly swiped at her chin with the back of her hand.

Ray slammed the door behind him and Kate held her breath until she heard the sound of the car engine fade away down the road. Despite being tired, Kate began cleaning up the kitchen, in case Ray came back to see what she was doing. Only once had she made the mistake of going back to bed after he left, and it had taken her a couple of days to get over the results of his temper.

She glanced at the clock. 5:45. He wouldn't come back now, because it would make him late for work and Wallace Lumber Company didn't take kindly to its loggers being late.

After cleaning the already clean house, Kate went out to do some weeding and check the progress of the vegetables in her garden. She looked across the emptiness surrounding their house and wished again that they had a neighbour or two. The day was rapidly getting warmer and a few drops of sweat formed on her brow as she leaned over pulling out an unwanted weed.

"Your garden looks good, muh dear."

Kate jumped at the unexpectedness of the scratchy voice.

"Sorry, muh dear, I didn't mean to startle yuh." The old lady dropped a basket on the ground, tipped her straw hat back and leaned on the fence. The hat immediately slipped down again.

"That's all right, Polly. I just didn't hear you comin'."

Polly giggled. "Most people don't."

"You haven't been around for a while," Kate continued. "Have you been ill?"

"Oh no, dearie. I never get ill. My herbs keep me healthy." She tipped her large straw hat back again and peered through her glasses. "Been thinkin' about you though. How have you been? You're lookin' a little peaked."

"I'm fine. Just ... a little ... you know," her voice trailed off.

"I know all right. That no good Ray Prentice been beatin' on yuh again." The old lady nodded her head. "Never was no good, that boy. Too bad yuh got yerself hooked up with him."

"Ray's all right. Just under a lot of pressure."

"You don't need to make excuses for him, Kate. He was bad as a boy and he's a bad man. Has a real mean streak in him, like his Daddy. Mean to animals and mean to humans. You're a right pretty gal and you don't need the likes of him beatin' on yuh."

"Ray doesn't ..."

"Don't tell me what Ray doesn't. I've seen the bruises even though you try to cover them up. Told yuh before, yuh oughtta run away. Get out of this little town. Find a good man somewhere."

"Well, it's hard ..."

"Gonna be a lot harder if you don't go. You'll end up in hospital or the morgue. Yuh need to disappear like Ray's ma."

"His ma disappeared? What happened? Ray never mentions his parents."

"He got good reason not to say anything. His no-good pa used to beat on his ma regular-like. Guess Ray figured that was the way families were. Then one day, his pa vanished, like he fell off the face of the earth or sumthin'. After that, Ray ran away from home. Sheriff thought maybe Ray had somethin' to do with it."

Kate shivered. "Do you think Ray killed his father?"

"No. Even though one was mean as the other, Charlie was much bigger. Ray was only twelve."

"And his ma?"

"Nobody knows exactly what happened to her. Might've left town or maybe went into hiding somewhere. That's what you need to do."

"Leave town? I couldn't do that. Besides, Ray would come after me and then ... well ... would you like to come in for some lemonade?" Belatedly, she remembered Ray's words. "Er, I mean, I could bring some lemonade out and we could drink it in the shade."

"No thanks, dearie. I've got to be gettin' back to Nellie. She's due to kid any time now, and I like to be there in case Mr. Coyote is watchin'. I brung yuh a nice dessert though. Made it special myself with some wildberries." Polly reached into her basket and handed a cloth-covered dish to Kate.

"Thank you so much, Polly. That's very kind. It doesn't have eggs in it, does it? I'm allergic to eggs you know."

"I plumb forgot about that, dearie. I'm so sorry. Maybe you can just give it to Ray then. He ain't allergic to anything except kindness."

"All right. I'll give it to him tonight. Thank you so much, Polly."

"You're welcome, dearie." Polly reached across the fence and pulled Kate to her in a hug. "You take care of yourself, and see that Ray gets that dessert. I'll come by another time."

Polly walked slowly away, limping slightly from the arthritis in her knees.

As always, Kate had Ray's supper ready before she heard the truck in the drive. He pushed the door open with a bang and dropped a bag of milk on the table. "There's your damn milk. Make sure you don't run out again. I hate makin' stops on my way home."

"I'm sorry, Ray. I'll remember. Supper's ready."

"It better be. I'm hungry."

After Ray finished the main course, Kate brought out the dessert.

"Where did this come from? Looks better than anything you ever make."

"Polly stopped by this morning."

"That stupid old woman. She gives me the creeps when I see her in town. You got to stop her comin' around here. I don't like it."

"She don't mean no harm, Ray. And it's not like I invite her or anythin'. She just comes."

Ray took a big spoonful of the pudding and berry sauce. "I'll say this much for the old woman. She makes a real nice pudding. This is good. I haven't had anything like this since ... for years. Why ain't you havin' some?"

"I can't. It's got eggs in it, and you know I'm allergic."

"Yeah, and you'd probably just get fatter anyway." Ray finished off the pudding, belched loudly and went into the living-room.

Kate began cleaning up. Over the noise of the television, she heard Ray holler. "Bring me a beer. And keep them comin' while the game's on."

Not being a football fan, Kate went into their bedroom to read, remembering to deliver a beer every so often. Eventually, Ray staggered into the bedroom, flopped on the bed and fell into a deep sleep. Kate removed his boots, threw a cover over him, and got into bed herself.

The alarm woke Kate from a sound sleep and she hurried to the kitchen to get things ready for Ray's breakfast. As she was pouring his coffee, she realized that she hadn't heard any sounds from the bedroom. She went to look. To her surprise, Kate saw Ray was still sleeping. She went over and shook him.

"Ray. Wake up! You're going to be late for work." There was no response.

"Ray? Ray!" She touched his face. It was cold. Throwing back the cover, she was assailed by the stench of excrement.

Kate screamed. "Oh my God! Ray!" There wasn't a sound loud enough to wake Ray Prentice.

Kate stood there trembling. She had no idea what to do. Ray had never allowed a phone in the house. She headed back to the kitchen and sat down hard, trying to think. Absentmindedly, she drank Ray's coffee.

A knock on the door made Kate jump. To her surprise, Polly was standing there.

"Oh Polly. Thank God. The most awful thing. Ray's dead. Or at least I think he is."

"Really. Well, maybe we'd best take a look." Kate led Polly to the bedroom.

Polly leaned over Ray, lifted an eyelid, then placed her fingers on his neck. "Yep, he's dead all right."

"I didn't know what to do. I guess I better get the police or somethin'."

Polly shook her head. "I don't think that's necessary, Kate. You've just been given a real opportunity here."

Kate frowned. "What do you mean?"

"This is your chance to get your things together and get out of this awful place. Start drivin' and don't look back."

"But, but ... I can't just leave Ray lying here."

"Leave everythin' to me, Kate. You just get packed up and get out. I'll take care of this." She steered Kate toward the dresser.

"But people are going to think I did something to him. And I didn't. I didn't."

"I know you didn't, darlin'. Don't worry about anything. There won't be no problem. You just leave and keep goin'."

With more urging from Polly, Kate gathered her few belongings and put them in the truck. She gave Polly a hug. "Will I see you sometime?"

"I don't think so, dearie. It's best that you never come this way again. You go find yourself some nice young man and forget all about Peaceful Valley. Go on now." She opened the truck door and Kate climbed in..

She put her hand out the window. "Thank you, Polly. I'll never forget you." Kate started out, waved and looked back one last time. The old lady was just standing in the drive, smiling.

Polly turned back to the house. She picked up a gas can and carried it inside. From the kitchen, she picked up Ray's lighter, went to the bedroom and poured gasoline over the bed.

At the doorway, she turned around and looked at the body. "I brought yuh into this world, Ray, and I've taken yuh out."

She flicked the lighter and threw it at the bed. Flames shot up to the ceiling.

"Now you can go rot in hell alongside yer pa."

Chapter 11

ABUSERS

"I can't imagine a mother killing her child, no matter how bad he was," Peter said, shaking his head.

Leona paused and looked at Derek. "Served him right, as far as I'm concerned. He deserved to die. Miserable bastard!"

"I have to agree, Leona," said Brent. "Hitting a woman is just not acceptable, and it seems there's a lot of wife abuse going around these days."

Joe's eyebrows raised as he tipped his head sideways. "Not only wife abuse, but husband abuse too. Women are just as capable of dishing it out as the men are."

"Joe, why are you so against women?" Kelly said. "First you talk about female serial killers and now women who abuse men."

"It's just a fact of life, that's all. Sure, fewer women beat up on their husbands, but I suspect that's because most women are afraid the husband will hit back. I've got nothing against women. In fact, I would be the first one to step in and turn the guy over to the cops."

"That could backfire on you, of course, Joe. We had a case in the office just recently of a woman trying to sue a man who stopped her boyfriend from beating her senseless."

"Were the charges dismissed, Brent?"

"Yes, they were, Laura. We convinced the judge that it was a frivolous case."

"Personally, I wouldn't mind playing the victim of a husband beater ... in a movie where it's not real." Danielle frowned. "Of course, that would mean wearing all sorts of gunk to make me look injured. I don't think I'd like that." She brightened. "Oh, and my public wouldn't like it at all." Danielle smiled, happy again.

"I think you should stick to glamorous roles, Danielle. They suit you better," said Brent.

Danielle smiled at him. "I agree, Brent. You are absolutely right."

"I'm a big fan of yours."

"Really?? How absolutely charming of you to say so, Brent. Which movie did you like best?"

"Probably the one where you took off the most clothes," said Angie. "It's obvious he isn't talking about the plot."

Carmen turned quickly to Angie. "You are a nasty woman, Mrs. Richardson, to say such a thing to this sweet young lady. Perhaps that is the problem. It is because she is young, yes? And beautiful. While you are ... old. "

Angie gasped. "I most certainly am not old! And age has nothing to do with it. She's simply an airhead with a great boob job," she retorted.

Dani's mouth fell open, speechless for once.

Brent hurried over. "I think you've had more than enough to drink, Angie. Please accept our apologies, Ms Davis. It's the booze talking. Derek, do you have a couch somewhere that Angie could lie down for a bit?"

"Of course."

"Don't touch me, Brent! I'm not going anywhere. And I certainly haven't had too much to drink." She shoved his hand off her shoulder and looked imploringly at Derek. "Derek, make him leave me alone."

Derek looked quickly between Angie and his wife. Leona glared at him and he looked again at Angie. "Um, uh, I, uh ..."

"I'm the one you need to listen to, Angie," Brent said, as he reached for her.

Angie's face contorted in anger."No! You need to listen to me. I'm not moving." Her shout bounced off the walls, and the assembled group, many with mouths agape, suddenly developed a great interest in the ceiling, the fireplace or the furniture.

Brent bit his lip. He could not hide the disgust from his face, and well aware of the discomfiture of the other guests, had no wish to make a further scene. He walked away. "Sorry folks," he said apologetically and resumed his seat.

Kelly patted Brent's arm and spoke quietly. "It's not your fault, Mr. Richardson. Don't worry about it."

The Colonel had no qualms about letting himself be heard by everyone. "Don't approve of people who can't hold their liquor. We had some fellows in the service like that. Had to kick them out. Fools!"

"Colonel, you shouldn't be harsh on people who are easily affected by alcohol. It is something in their DNA that makes them susceptible to the influence of liquor," said Carmen. "Besides, I don't think it's the alcohol that's the problem."

"So you're a ..." the Colonel snorted, "psychic AND a doctor, madame?"

Before Carmen could reply, Derek spoke up. "Ah...I think we're about ready for one more story. I've got one I heard from an acquaintance."

Everyone drew in a breath and settled back, except for Brent who kept watching Angie.

Chapter 12

ANOTHER LIFE

Marcie threw her arms high in the air in a classic 'v' shape soaking up the lusty waves of testosterone that washed over her naked body. The applause and cheering continued after she made her exit. Sam Torino was waiting in the wings.

"Great show, Marcie. They really love you. Don't ever leave us, babe."

"I can't stay young forever, Sam." Marcie laughed as she entered the cubbyhole that Sam called a dressing-room. She grabbed a towel and wiped the sweat from her torso and under her long blonde hair. "I wish I didn't sweat so much."

"Why you keep coming back to this joint beats me," Darla said, squinting at Marcie's reflection. "It's not like they couldn't run this place without you. I thought you took that course so's you'd be like regular people. And what about Harry?"

Marcie wondered how she could explain to Darla that she actually liked stripping, or at least the results of stripping. She loved the power it gave her over men, the feeling of having something they wanted but couldn't have, the knowledge that all of them desired her. It gave her an orgasmic high. It was like sex without the mess.

Aloud, she said, "Darla, it's kind of hard to explain. I like my daytime job, but it's pretty routine, you know? Not only that, it doesn't pay me that much, and I intend to have lots of money before I get ..." Marcie choked back her words as she looked at Darla. Under all that make-up, Darla's face looked much older than her twenty-eight years. Late nights, smoking, drinking and bouncing from guy to guy had left their mark. Marcie had no intention of looking like forty in another five years.

"Well, you know ..." she finished lamely.

"What's Harry say about it? I thought he wanted you to quit." Darla was really in a peevish mood, especially since Sam had replaced her picture out front with Marcie's.

"He's not too happy, but he'll just have to learn to be patient." Marcie removed the false eyelashes and applied cream to her face.

"I think he's a great guy. Wouldn't mind if his slippers found their way under my bed." Darla put a nurse's cap on and pinned it in place.

"Yeah, Harry's okay."

Darla turned and faced Marcie. "I think he's more than okay. If I was you, I'd be hangin' on real tight to him. If you don't watch out, somebody else'll come along and take him away." Darla took a last look in the mirror then headed to the door. She turned back to Marcie and straightened her nurse's uniform. "Remember what I said. There's lotsa women looking for a guy like Harry." The door banged behind her.

Marcie sighed as she finished dressing. Having to put up with petty jealousy was the worst part of being at the Purple Onion. Like it was her fault that Sam gave her top billing.

"Hey, Marce. You decent?" Harry's voice called through the door.

Marcie adjusted a black tunic over her leggings. "Yeah." *Why is he afraid of seeing me naked or half-dressed here?* Marcie couldn't figure out. *God knows he's seen me enough times before we started dating. Come to think of it, he always wants the lights out when we go to bed together. Weird.*

"You lovely, sweetheart," Harry kissed her on the cheek.

Marcie didn't have to look at Harry to know he was wearing black slacks, neatly pressed and a blue-toned sweater. It was his regular style. "Thanks. I'm ready," she said. "Let's go."

Harry started the car. Marcie closed her eyes and leaned back on the headrest.

"I didn't get a chance to tell you, Marce. I talked to Stan the Man yesterday, and it looks pretty promising that I'll be getting a promotion before too long. Carter told me that Bill Waters is thinking of retiring in the next few months." Bill Waters was head of Carter Chemicals Eastern Division Accounting Department.

"Did Mr. Carter tell you you'd be taking Bill's place?"

"Not exactly. But I think it was sort of understood."

"Hmmm."

"What does that mean?" Harry stole a glance at her. "I thought you'd be happy. This would mean we could get married as early as next year."

Marcie kept her eyes closed and thought of marriage to Harry. It would be predictable, safe, comfortable. Kids, probably. Wasn't that what she wanted? Yes, but ... it seemed like there was another word missing, and it didn't take her long to come up with it. Boring. Could she handle the boredom? It was for sure she would have to give up stripping. Sex with Harry was okay but it would never give her the high that she got on the stage. Probably no single man could do that.

"Are you sleeping?"

"What? Oh no, sorry. I was just thinking. Stan Carter has a habit of letting you think one thing while he intends something else, sort of deceptive, you know? He would have made a good actor. In fact, sometimes I wonder if he wasn't in little theatre or something when he was younger. He is always so dramatic about everything."

"Well, I'm pretty sure about this. Keep your eyes open next week and see if you see anything that might be some kind of confirmation...you know, office memo from Bill or something."

"I'll let you know, Harry, but don't get your hopes up, unless Mr. Carter tells you point blank that you're getting the job."

The following Friday, Stan Carter came hurrying into the office looking decidedly upset. "Marcie, come in my office please ... and close the door. Please sit down." Stan ran his hand over his balding head and dropped into the huge leather chair behind his desk.

Marcie was puzzled. "What's wrong, Mr. Carter?"

Carter lit a cigar. "Marcie, you know my school chum, Matthew Fellows, is coming in today from LeHavre Biotech in St. Louis."

"Yes, I made the dinner arrangements for you and Mrs. Carter to take him to the Starlight Room."

"Right. Right. So you did." He placed the cigar in an ash-tray. "Marcie, I don't know how to say this. I need a favour of you."

"Of course. What can I do?"

His words came tumbling out. "Helen took really ill in the night and I had to take her to the hospital. I'm going back there as soon as I make a couple of calls. The point is, obviously we can't make the dinner tonight with Matt, and I'm wondering... now I realize this is a last minute thing and I hate to impose... but I'm wondering if you could go to dinner with him. I need to get a package to him." His eyes were opened wide, pleading. "I know this is asking a lot..."

"Mr. Carter. Mr. Carter," Marcie broke in. "Yes, that's fine. I can do that. No problem."

Stan let out the breath he had been holding and picked up his cigar. "Thank you so much, Marcie. You have no idea how worried I've been, what with Helen and this meeting and... Well, thank you. I'll pay you for your time, of course. Tell the restaurant to charge it to the company account. Oh, and here ...." He jumped to his feet, removed his wallet from a back pocket, and held out a hundred dollar bill. "Take this for cab fare or whatever. And here's a key for our company penthouse where he's staying." He put the cigar down again.

"Company penthouse?"

"Oh. I guess you haven't heard about it yet. We maintain a penthouse in Bayview Towers for visiting clients. Matt will be staying there. Do you know where that is?"

Marcie's eyes opened wide. *Company penthouse? That is a surprise.* "Yes, it overlooks the bay. Don't worry about anything, Mr. Carter. I'll see that Mr. Fellows gets the package. What's wrong with your wife?"

Carter gave her a blank stare. "Uh, we don't know yet. They're running some tests today. I've got to be with her."

It crossed Marcie's mind that if he didn't calm down, he would end up in a bed beside her. "Mr. Carter...I'm sure she'll be fine. You make your calls and don't worry any more about Mr. Fellows."

Returning to her desk, Marcie's fingers drummed as she tried to decide what to wear for the evening. Mr. Fellows would be an aging chemist like Stan Carter and the other test tube nuts, so it wouldn't matter much anyway. Those guys couldn't see anything unless it was under a microscope.

Stan Carter came out of his office. He appeared noticeably calmer. "Thanks again, Marcie. Tell Matt I'll call him tomorrow. Oh!" Stan turned back from the door. He smiled. "Be sure and leave a good tip at the Starlight."

"I will. Say hello to your wife for me."

Marcie buzzed Alex Simpson, head of the typing pool. "Alex, Mr. Carter and I are both going to be gone for the rest of the day, so just take messages for us, okay? Great. Have a good weekend."

At seven o'clock that night, Marcie slipped the card key into the elevator at Bayview Towers and pushed the button for the penthouse floor. She glanced at her several reflections and thought that the blue and silver pantsuit had been a good choice to go with the French roll into which the hairdresser had twisted her hair.

Marcie stepped off the elevator and into the elegant quiet of the penthouse, where huge vases of flowers were reflected several times in the ornate mirrors lining the walls. She inhaled the delightful floral scents and debated whether to knock or let herself in. Checking her watch, she decided it would be better to knock as Matthew Fellows should be there by now.

A tall, black-haired man opened the door. "Miss Robertson, I presume."

Marcie was momentarily taken aback. The man before her was over six feet tall, under thirty years old and his after-shave was a heart-stopper . Her eyebrows rose causing a slight furrow in her forehead. "Mr. Fellows?"

"At your service." He bowed slightly and stepped back. " Please come in."

"But you can't be Mr. Fellows. You're too young. I mean, you went to school with Mr. Carter. I expected ... you're ..." She cursed herself inwardly for babbling.

He laughed. "Ah! I see you didn't get my message. I'm James Fellows. My father couldn't come and sent me in his place." He smiled.

Marcie hesitated at the door. Was she still supposed to go to dinner? "Oh, I see. Uh, well, I have the package here for you."

"Thanks. I'll just put it away and grab my jacket."

"Uh ..." Marcie felt like a fool. He was so much at ease and she was as nervous as a skunk in a room full of tomato juice.

He stopped and turned back. "We are going to eat, right?"

"Well, I ..., yes."

"Oh good. I was afraid for a minute that we weren't going to have dinner, and I'm starving." He slipped a dinner jacket over his white shirt. "Shall we go?"

James Fellows turned out to be as charming as he was good-looking. After telling Marcie that he was the Business Manager for LeHavre Biotech, he said he would much rather concentrate on the food and her company than talk business. They quickly became quite comfortable with each other as they discovered common interests in jogging, tennis and swimming.

Dinner seemed to be over much too soon, from Marcie's point of view and, she hoped, James'. Before leaving the restaurant, James called a cab for each of them. After she entered the taxi, he leaned in and gave her a quick kiss, giving her even more reason to wish the evening wasn't over.

Marcie's mind was in a whirl. The last thing she had expected was to have dinner at the Starlight Room with a handsome young man. A rich, handsome young man. What a pity he lived four hours away. Sleep did not come quickly, and it didn't help that the phone insisted that she wake up early Saturday morning. Trying to surface from a deep sleep, Marcie groggily picked up the receiver. "H'lo."

"Marcie. It's Harry."

Marcie groaned. "Harry. What do you want? What time is it?"

"About nine." His voice was petulant. "I tried to call you last night. You didn't answer."

"Oh yeah. I was out." Mr. Carter asked me to deliver a package to someone staying at the company penthouse. Can we talk about this later?"

"Well, I guess. How about if I come over? I'll make you breakfast."

"Harry, I don't give a rat's ass about breakfast. I want to sleep."

"Oh. Was it a late night meeting? Who was it? Did you go out somewhere or something?"

Marcie's annoyance grew. "What are you, the Neighborhood Watch or something?" She sighed deeply. "Harry...I'll see you tonight, okay? Good-bye." Marcie hung up quickly to end the interrogation.

That night, it took some time to convince Harry that the previous evening was just a business meeting, particularly as Marcie wasn't so sure about that herself.

Monday morning came and with it, two dozen red roses delivered to Marcie's desk. It seemed that James Fellows was also unsure.

Stan Carter came in looking very happy and stopped to admire the roses. "Seems you made a good impression on James, Marcie. He called me yesterday."

"Did he? I hope his report was good. How's your wife, Mr. Carter?"

"What? Oh, uh, my wife. Yes. She's fine. Just a little indigestion, that's all."

All that fuss for indigestion? Really! "Oh. Well, that must be a relief."

The office grapevine was humming about the roses and it wasn't long before Harry appeared at Marcie's desk. "So it's true."

Marcie groaned inwardly. "What's true, Harry?"

"This." He jerked his thumb at the flowers.

"Mr. Fellows sent flowers." She placed her hands flat on her desk. "So what? He was just being nice, that's all." Marcie hoped what she really thought didn't show.

Harry crossed his arms and curled his lip. "Yeah right."

"Harry, I have work to do." She pulled a file folder out of a desk drawer.

He scowled. “I don’t like it,” he said, his voice rising four decibels.

Marcie looked around at her coworkers, who immediately found something of great importance on their desks. “Harry. You’re making a scene. Leave.”

“Oh, good morning, Harry.” Carter stepped out of his office in a cloud of cigar smoke. “Can I help you with something?”

“Uh, no thanks, Mr. Carter. I was just ... uh, leaving.”

Flowers from James arrived two more times that week and by Friday night, Harry was in a very sour mood. He sulked through their dinner date and drank more than he should have. Marcie insisted that the flowers didn’t mean anything, but her heart wasn’t in the lie because she was anticipating with excitement the next week when she would deliver another package to James, a fact she had no intention of telling Harry.

When Marcie finished her routine at the Purple Onion on Saturday night, she heard Harry and Darla having a heart-to-heart conversation in the dressing-room. Darla’s voice carried through the partially opened door.

“She’s not the only fish in the sea, Harry.”

Harry must be bending Darla’s ear with a tale of woe. The conversation ended abruptly when Marcie came in.

The third time Marcie brought a package to the penthouse, she found that James had ordered in dinner from the Maison D’Or. Sexual energy was palpable in the air and neither one seemed to have much interest in the food. They rose from the table together and with no apparent movement, Marcie ended up in his arms. It was only a short walk to the bedroom and both were naked by the time they reached the bed.

Marcie's affair with James Fellows bloomed over the next few weeks as she continued to see him and deliver a package each Friday night. The more things heated up with James, the angrier Harry grew. Finally, to Marcie's relief, he refused to speak to her at all. He became very despondent, particularly when the rumour mill started spreading the word that the son of a friend of Mr. Carter's was going to be hired as the new head of the Divisional Accounting Department.

On an overcast Friday, Marcie awoke with a headache that bothered her all morning. She decided to take the afternoon off and rest up at the penthouse before her date with James. As she exited the building, Harry accosted her.

He grabbed her shoulder. "Is it true?" he asked belligerently.

Marcie shrugged off his hand. "Is what true?"

"Some dickhead friend of old man Carter's is being brought in for the Divisional Manager job?"

"I have no idea, Harry."

"Bullshit!" He grabbed her arms. "You're thick as thieves with Carter and his cronies. You must know." His face was only inches away from Marcie's and waves of alcohol washed over her.

"Take your hands off me - you're hurting me!. I don't know anything, Harry. Get away from me." Marcie tried to shove him, but he was too strong.

"Whatsa matter? I'm not good enough for you now that you've got some rich guy hanging around."

"You're drunk, Harry. Get away!" He released his grip. "And stay away from me." Shaking, Marcie hurried to her car.

"Someday you'll be sorry, bitch!"

Marcie was still upset when she arrived home. She took some aspirin and lay down. A couple of hours later, she felt considerably better, and brightened up as she readied her things to take to the apartment for her evening with James.

While driving to the penthouse, Marcie thought a car was following her, but put it down to the nervous upset she had felt from her encounter with Harry. She placed the package on the coffee table and lit the fireplace. The glow reflected in the dark windows overlooking Shadow Bay.

She lay back against the chesterfield cushions and idly looked at the package, not for the first time wondering what was in it. She had queried James, but he said he wasn't interested in his father's side of the business and never opened it. In the bouncing flames, the package took on a life of its own, beckoning fingers of yellow and red inviting her inspection. Marcie picked it up. She could probably open it and reseal it. The serpent hissed in her ear telling her to do it.

Marcie undid the string and very carefully slid her nail under the tape. Inside was a box which she opened carefully. A large plastic bag full of white powder lay inside some tissue paper. "Oh my God." Marcie was not a user but she had seen enough heroin and coke to recognize a drug when she saw it. She and James were pawns in some kind of drug deal.

Marcie raced to the phone and called James' cell but there was no answer. She left an urgent message on his voice mail, and contacted information for Biotech's number and called to check when he had left.

"I'm sorry. There is no Mr. Fellows here."

"What? I don't understand. James Fellows? Or how about Matthew Fellows?"

"No, I'm sorry. You must have the wrong number."

"But I can't have. This is Biotech, right, and they both work there."

"Sorry."

Marcie dropped the phone on the table. With the hammers pounding incessantly in her head, Marcie had difficulty thinking clearly as so many scenarios swirled through her mind. The phone rang and she grabbed it as swiftly as a drowning person would grab a lifeline. "Hello?"

"Marcie. It's James. What's the matter?"

"Oh James. It's...I've got this horrible headache and Harry and we're... I just tried to call you at Biotech and they said you didn't work there."

A slight pause.

"You must have had the wrong number. Where did you get it?"

"From information."

"Did you remember to say LeHavre Biotech, because if you didn't, they probably gave you Biogage Industries instead of LeHavre. I'm sorry you have a headache, honey. Is that what you called me about?"

"Oh. Yes, that's probably it. No, no. I mean...James, do you know what is in those packages I've been giving you?"

"No. I told you. I don't involve myself with my father's end of the business. Why?"

"Well, I did something I shouldn't and I opened it." She heard an indrawn breath.

"And what did you find?"

"Drugs." Marcie's free arm swung frantically in the air. "I don't know if it's cocaine or heroin, but it's white powder and I'm sure it's a drug." She leaned on the table held her forehead. "James, we're in big trouble. We can't keep doing this. If the police find out..." She sat up straight, frowned and stared into the mocking flames.

"Okay, calm down, Marcie. Maybe it isn't a drug, but just some kind of powder compound. I'll get in touch with my Dad and ask him, okay? You know these chemists. They're always messing around trying to build a better mousetrap."

"Do you really think so?"

"Oh sure. I'll find out and be able to tell you when I get there tonight. Why don't you just lie down and rest and try to get rid of that headache? I'll see you in a few hours. Okay, hon?"

"Okay. I'll try. See you later then."

Marcie was far from convinced but decided to take his advice and lie down on the couch. Her fitful sleep was interrupted by the insistent buzzing of the front entrance intercom. To her disgust, Harry's slurred voice responded to her query.

"Go away, Harry. I don't want to see you."

"Marcie, I'm sorry for what I said earlier. I just want to apologize. I've brought you something."

"Apology accepted, Harry, but I'm not letting you in. I'm resting, Please leave."

"But Marcie..."

"No, Harry. Goodbye." Marcie waited a moment, half expecting the buzzer to sound again, but all was quiet. She saw by her watch that it would be a few hours before James would arrive and the thought of a nice hot bath sounded most appealing.

Marcie gratefully eased herself into the soothing water, laid her head back, closed her eyes and tried not to think of anything. She was nearly asleep when a slight sound made her look at the bathroom door. It was slowly opening.

"Who's there? James? Is that you?"

A figure entered the room holding a revolver. Marcie's eyes widened at the sight of the intruder. The gun fired twice and Marcie's startled face slowly slipped beneath the crimsoning water.

Retrieving the package from the coffee table, the intruder left the building quietly and drove to the pier at Shadow Bay. The gun made a small splash as it entered the water.

He dialled a number on his cell. "Thanks for the call, James. It's done. Send in the clean-up crew."

As the killer drove off, there was just one thought occupying his mind. He lit a cigar. On Monday, he would have to advertise for a new secretary.

Chapter 13

WEIRDOS EVERYWHERE

"Whoo ... I didn't expect that," said Greg eyes wide.

"Oooooh ... I would LOVE to play that role," said Dani. "Greg, do you think we could get some writers interested in writing a screenplay? Of course, I'm a little shy about stripping. I'd need a body suit. And the bathtub scene would have to be done tastefully."

Angie snorted. She had seen a couple of Dani's movies.

Greg nodded. "I'm sure I can talk to some people, Dani, when we get back to LA."

"I think people who strip are kind of in the line of fire, so to speak, of the weirdos out there," Kelly said.

"I don't think you have to be a stripper to run into weirdos," Angie said. "They're everywhere. And sometimes circumstances bring us face to face with them. In fact, the story I'm going to share will illustrate that. Would you like me to tell it now, Derek?"

"Certainly. Go right ahead."

"I'll be surprised if you can remember it," Leona said.

"There's nothing wrong with my memory, Leona. Sorry if you're having trouble with yours. I understand it comes with aging." Angie smiled.

"Oh, really. Perhaps it's something like drinking too much. Makes your skin look old and wrinkled."

Anger clouded Angie's face but before she could retort, Derek spoke up. "Uh ... the story, Angie?"

Laura whispered to Joe, "It'll be a wonder if those two don't have a hair-pulling contest before the end of the evening."

Joe smiled and nodded.

"Okay. I can't remember where I read this ..."

"What were you saying about aging and memory loss?" Leona said sweetly.

Derek glared at Leona. "Drop it!"

"... but I certainly remember the story." Angie turned her back to Leona.

Chapter 14

BREAKDOWN

Vicki Lamb watched a big man lumber out of the gas station toward her car. A checkered, flannel shirt blew out like bat wings on either side of him. His ears stuck out from between longish hair imprisoned under a baseball cap which was pulled low on his forehead, virtually obscuring his features in the semi-dark.

He pulled the hose off the pump and peered in her window. "Fill 'er up?" he asked, his breath an unpleasant smell of cheap whiskey and cigarette smoke. "Cash only."

"Yes, please ...", Vicki noted the name tag on his shirt as she leaned away from the odour, "Joe. My gas gauge isn't working so I'm not sure how much it will take."

He inserted the pump and nodded. "Wouldn't be a good idea to run out of gas at night on this road. Quite a ways to another station, and they'd likely be closed by the time you got there. Don't stay open late in the country. Just gettin' ready to close up myself."

"Yes, well, I thought I was taking a shortcut. Didn't work out that way."

Joe made a noise which Vicki decided was a laugh. "This road ain't no shortcut to anywhere," he said, shaking his head.

He seemed to be taking a long time filling the tank. *Must be pretty empty.* Vicki riffled through the bills in her wallet, picking out $50.00, just in case. She looked in the rear view mirror and watched until she saw him draw back from the car, hang up the hose and screw the gas cap back in place.

As he passed her window, he said, "Gonna check the oil."

"The oil's okay."

Joe seemed not to hear her as he continued to the front of the car. Vicki shrugged her shoulders, popped the hood and watched through the small gap as Joe disappeared, then straightened up with the oil stick in his hand. A minute later, he slammed down the hood, grabbed the long handled sponge and washed off her windshield. He dropped the sponge back into the container and came to the window. "Oil's okay. That'll be $38.50."

Vicki handed him two twenties. "Keep the change." she said. "How far do I have to go before hooking up with the interstate?"

Thinking seemed to be a slow process with Joe. "Ummm, must be about 100 or so miles as the crow flies. That's if a crow wanted to go to the Interstate." Joe chuckled in his throat at his own joke and stuffed the money in his jeans pocket.

Vicki smiled. "Bit of a drive, I guess. Okay, thanks Joe."

"Unhunh."

Full darkness had descended by the time Vicki pulled out of the gas station. She turned the CD up, trusting that Rod Stewart's loud music would keep her awake. Tall trees hugged the side of the road, as if they were waiting to absorb energy from any living thing that happened to pass by.

Rod was in the middle of telling a sweet young thing that tonight was the night, when he was cut off in mid-note by a loud cough, the last sound the car engine made before stalling.

"What the hell!" Vicki managed to steer the car closer to the side of the road before the forward momentum stopped the vehicle. She took a minute to calm her nerves, and tried to start the car again. Nothing.

She pulled out her cell phone. To her dismay, she discovered she was in a dead zone. "Damn! Now what am I supposed to do?" she said aloud, thumping the steering wheel.

Vicki grabbed a flashlight from under the seat and stepped out of the car. The scene was not encouraging. Nothing but darkness and watching trees. Walking back 20 miles to the gas station didn't seem like a very good option, so she decided to go forward in the hopes of finding a house.

As she trudged along, Vicki swung her flashlight from side to side. Suddenly, the light reflected off something silver, a few feet down the road and she quickened her pace. As she came closer, Vicki realized it was a rural mailbox. "Thank God," she breathed. Peering through the darkness beyond the mailbox, she spotted a wrought iron gate hanging on one hinge. She pushed it open and squeezed through.

Broken concrete slabs led the way up toward the house, its dark features now visible in the encroaching beam of the flashlight. No interior lights offered any welcome and Vicki shivered as she stepped onto the sagging porch. *I hope they don't mind being awakened*, The door quivered slightly under her loud knock. She waited a polite minute, knocked several times more and was about to give up when the door finally opened, revealing a gnome-like old woman holding a hurricane lamp.

"Hello? Who is it?" Her voice was raspy as if she hadn't used it for a long time.

"I'm sorry to disturb you. I'm Vicki Lamb. There's a problem with my car," she said waving an arm toward the road, "and I'm wondering if I might use your phone." Vicki shivered again.

A sandpaper scraping-on-metal noise came from the old woman's mouth. "Oh dearie, we don't have a phone, but - come in, come in. It's cold out there."

Vicki hesitated. "I really need to call someone. Perhaps I could go to a neighbor."

"I'm afraid the next house is about five miles away. I think you'd best come in. My son will be able to help you."

Drawing in a deep breath of courage and ignoring the hairs rising on her neck, Vicki stepped through the door. The house smelled stale, as if no fresh air had been allowed to enter its walls in a very long time.

"Come this way, dear. I'll make you a nice cup of tea." As the old lady turned, the lamp cast long shadows on the walls of the gloomy hallway.

"Oh no, thanks. I don't want to put you to any trouble. If your son could just..."

"No trouble at all. It will be lovely to have some company. I haven't had anyone for a long time, Miss Lamb."

"Call me Vicki, please," she said loudly to the old lady's rapidly retreating back.

The light from a propane lamp in the ceiling revealed a surprisingly large kitchen with an old wooden slab table and two stuffed chairs placed in front of the window. At odds with the propane fixture and furniture were the very modern stainless steel refrigerator and matching stove.

"Sit down, dear," said the old lady. After plugging in the kettle, she put two cups on the counter. "Oh my," she said. "I have forgotten my manners. My name is Annie Ball. It is so nice to have you visit, dear."

In the glow of the lamp, Annie's face looked like an apple doll, all wrinkled and brown. Gray hair and little granny glasses completed the picture. Her thin, almost frail, body was lost inside a voluminous flannelette nightgown, over which she had thrown a beautiful crocheted dark red shawl.

"It's nice to meet you, Mrs. Ball. I'm sorry to have interrupted your sleep, and I really appreciate your letting me come in when it's so late."

"Don't worry, dear. I wasn't asleep yet. Besides, we don't usually have visitors at this time of night, so I figured it had to be someone in trouble. I always like to take good care of anyone who comes by."

"That's a beautiful shawl you're wearing, Mrs. Ball."

"You like it? Thank you, my dear. I made it myself." Annie pulled the shawl off her shoulders and handed it to Vickie.

"A lovely design, and the colour is so vibrant. I've never seen any quite like it." She handed the shawl back to Annie.

Annie chuckled. "You likely never will. It's a special dye that I make myself from poppies and a special, secret ingredient." She smiled and swung the shawl over her back.

Vicki's eyes travelled to the shelves beside the stove which displayed an extensive collection of spices and herbs, all neatly arranged with names facing out.

"I see you looking at my spice racks. Do you like to cook?"

"Not really. I mean, I try, but I'm not very good."

"I imagine you cook quite well. The secret is in the spices and knowing which ones to use for different pieces of meat. My son and I are excellent cooks. We supply gourmet foods to a couple of Five Star restaurants in Tacohonga."

"Oh, then you must have an extensive garden to grow a lot of vegetables in the summer."

"Vegetables? Oh yes, of course. And we have poultry too. And meat. My Priest Stew is an especial favourite with the customers. I'll probably be making some more tomorrow. Do you live near here, dear?"

"Not really. I live in Richmond, but I was visiting friends in Todson. This looked like a shortcut so I thought I'd try it."

"You've come a long way then. You must be hungry. I have some of my ultra tender McAllister chops in the freezer if you would like me to make you something."

"Oh no, thank you. I picked up dinner a while back."

"Well, perhaps some cookies then. They will go nicely with our tea. Oh! Water's boiling." Annie took down a tea canister and placed four heaping spoons of loose tea into a large, flower-bedecked teapot.

Vicki watched as the gnarled, bony hands shakily placed a plate of cookies on the table, along with two napkins beautifully monogrammed with the initials CAB. "There we are. Help yourself."

"Would you like me to pour the tea?" Vicki asked, envisioning liquid spilling everywhere.

"How kind of you, dear. Yes, please. My hands are not too steady these days, especially when I get excited."

"You have only two cups here. Won't your son be joining us?"

"Actually, Jonathan isn't here at the moment, but he should be home fairly soon. What exactly is wrong with your car?"

"I don't know really. It just stalled. I thought maybe I could call that garage where I gassed up a while back."

"Oh, you mean Cousin Joe's place. Jonathan's likely shut down and on his way home by now. We'll get him to check your car for you when he gets here." Annie hesitated. "It would probably be better in the daylight though. You would be most welcome to stay overnight if you wish."

"Oh goodness, no. I could never impose on you like that," Vicki said, sipping her tea.

"You would not be imposing at all, dear. We have plenty of space for you. The choice is yours, however. While we're waiting, why don't we go sit in the parlor. The chairs are more comfortable and we can drink our tea by a fire."

Picking up the hurricane lamp again, Annie led Vicki into a small room off the kitchen. Two overstuffed green chairs set on either side of a brick fireplace, took up most of the floor space. The room was cold and musty. "You're probably wondering why I use the lamp instead of turning on the lights," Annie said.

"I did, rather."

"It's an old habit. I like the electricity for cooking and things, but I love the lamplight. It just seems so much nicer. Reminds me of when I was a little girl." Annie set the lamp on the hearth and busied herself lighting the kindling already laid in the grate.

An avid reader, Vicki's attention was drawn to a large lawyer's bookcase standing in the corner. After placing the teacups on a tiny table, she examined the titles through the glass doors and, to her surprise, found quite a diverse selection: 'War and Peace' fought for space between 'Treasure Island' and 'Tom Sawyer', 'The Caine Mutiny' rubbed shoulders with 'How to do

Almost Everything' and "Butchering Made Easy" stood in the middle of a dozen cookbooks.

She straightened up and shivered. "You have quite an assortment of books here, Mrs. Ball."

"Oh yes. I love to read. Come sit down, my dear. The fire will heat us up in no time. This is so nice. I don't get to use the parlor very often."

Vicki sat down. The tea was hot and warmed up her insides. She held her hands out to the blazing fire. "This is really very nice of you, Mrs. Ball." She yawned.

"You see, you are tired. Don't worry, if you doze off, I'll wake you when Jonathan comes in, that is, if I don't doze myself," Annie cackled. "Happens a lot when you get old."

Vicki drank some more. "I noticed the monogram on the napkins - CAB. Were those your husband's initials?"

"Can I tell you a secret, dear?" Annie leaned forward confidentially. "I was never married. But when I was young, having a baby without a father was a big disgrace to the family and enough to get you thrown out of the community. So I left home, came here where no one knew me and pretended that my husband had died."

She sat back and smiled. "Those are my initials. I just added the 'C' as a little joke. I never did get married. Couldn't find the right man. Raising Jonathan properly gave me plenty to do anyway."

Something nagged at Vicki's memory. "Didn't you call Joe at the gas station your cousin?"

"Oh. Yes. It's just a nickname. Everyone calls him that."

Vicki yawned again. "I'm sorry. I seem to be getting very sleepy. It must be the heat."

"Just rest dear. I talk too much anyway."

"Not at all. I enjoy listening to you, but it was a long drive and I guess I'm more tired that I realized."

Vicki rested her head against the back of the chair and, wrapped in the warmth of the room, closed her eyes. She thought she could hear a murmur of voices, but her consciousness refused to be aroused. She drifted into a very deep sleep.

What felt like only seconds later, Vicki woke, feeling a coldness numbing her body. Her legs seemed paralyzed. Her arms, too, wouldn't move. She blinked several times trying to clear the fog in her brain. Her eyes rebelled against the bright light that penetrated her eyelids and Vicki turned her head to the left in an attempt to get away from it. Her mind had difficulty processing the row of gleaming knives in velvet boxes set beside a power saw, all of which were arranged neatly on a workbench.

Her eyes glanced up above the table, where two shelves were filled with red blobs that looked like liver or kidneys. Horror set in and her eyes opened wide when she saw the row of pickled eyeballs that stared unseeingly at her from the third shelf.

Full awareness washed over her like a cold shower as Vicki realized she was lying naked on a metal table, her wrists and ankles bound by leather straps. Panic set in. She screamed and thrashed about trying to loosen her bindings.

As she swung her head to the right, she saw a heavy, muscular man staring at her with the dead eyes of a hungry shark. Gone was the baseball cap and the flannel shirt was now covered by a full-length rubber apron. "Joe?"

Beside him stood Annie watching Vicki as a cat watches a mouse that it knows can't escape. "Quickly, Jonathan. She's awake. Put the duct tape over her mouth. You know I don't like to hear them scream," Annie said.

"What's going on? No! Wait! Please! No!" Vicki thrashed her head from side to side to no avail. With an evil smile, Jonathan swiftly secured the tape over her open mouth. Her eyes widened in terror as Jonathan picked up a meat cleaver and once more stood beside her.

"Hurry up, dear. My mouth is watering," Annie's rusty voice urged.

"Yes, mother."

Still smiling, Jonathan lifted the cleaver over his head and brought it down with a whack, severing Vicki's right leg at the knee. Her muffled scream faded away as her eyes closed and body sagged.

Annie removed the one ankle restraint and deftly picked up the leg with a plastic bag.

"Don't forget to let all the blood drain out before you put the rest of the meat in the freezer, Jonathan." She wrapped some plastic around Vicki's leg. "I'll let this drip out into the sink and then put it on the stove. I can hardly wait. It's been so long since we've had leg of Lamb." Annie's riotous laughter filled the room.

Chapter 15

TENSIONS RISING

"Eeeeew," Dani said, wrinkling up her face. "Gross!"

Angie laughed. "Personally, I like the dark humour."

"That doesn't surprise me," Leona said. "Just indicative of the kind of things you probably think are funny."

"Oh come on. Even YOU have to admit that 'leg of Lamb' is pretty funny. Of course, I also like the gourmet foods being supplied to Five Star restaurants. Priest stew?" Angie laughed again. "And did anyone pick up on the little old lady's name?"

"Annie," said Kelly.

"Yes, but Annie what?"

"Annie Ball, I think it was," Peter said.

"Right. But do you remember her monogrammed napkins - CAB? Think about that. C. Annie Ball," Angie said slowly, then again faster. "C. Annieball. Cannieball. Cannibal, get it?" Angie laughed again.

Several people groaned. Dani looked puzzled. "See Annie Ball? I don't understand. She wasn't crying." She looked to Carmen for help.

"I'll explain later."

"Oh for Pete's sake. You people need to loosen up. Have another drink. I'll join you. You can never have too much of a good thing, right Derek?" Angie said, placing her hand on his chest.

"There are some things that aren't good for you at all," Leona said, slapping Angie's arm away.

Angie's eyes blazed and she lifted her hand to strike Leona, but Derek stopped her in mid-air. "Don't!"

Brent crossed the room and took Angie's arm. "Perhaps you'd better come sit with us."

"Good idea. This side of the room has a definitely unpleasant aroma in it." Angie looked pointedly at Leona. "How can you stand being so near to the stink, Derek? Aren't you afraid it might rub off?"

Brent held her arm until she collapsed into a chair close to Kelly. "Get me another drink like a good boy, darling," Angie said, tilting her head back to look up at Brent. He sighed and walked over to the bar.

Kelly and Peter exchanged glances and raised eyebrows. "Aiding and abetting?" Kelly whispered.

"Pretty much what I was thinking." Peter nodded his head.

"Perhaps you would care to hear a different type of story," Greg said. "This is one I heard from a fellow Californian."

Derek nodded. "Go ahead, Greg."

Brent returned and handed Angie her drink.

"By all means, Greg. Carry on." She raised her glass in salute.

"All right. I'll tell it in his own words."

Chapter 16

IN THE BLINK OF AN EYE

I live high on a hill overlooking one of the largest cities in the world. It sprawls far beneath me, a tribute to man's determination to control the wilderness and those engineers who made it possible. In sharp contrast to the mostly white, man-made structures, the dark green of the trees climbing upward from the valley is a reminder of the way it used to be, before man changed the face of the land.

I have a dream. Oh, not the visionary type which will bring peace to mankind, but rather the tumultuous, disturbing dream that haunts me in the middle of the night. It has come to me for a few years at different times, but of late, it has tormented my sleep nightly. I have to hope that this dream does not become a reality.

What I dream is that the city disappears and I am gripped with an inexplicable terror from a menace I cannot see. I wake in a cold sweat, my body twisted in the sheets. Each morning, I stand on the patio drinking my coffee, imagining what it would be like if that city were not there and trying to envision some reason why it would simply disappear. My dream does not show destruction, just a vanishing.

I mentioned this dream to my best friend Mickey. He offered the same solution he always does no matter what my problem. "Jackie-boy, you need to get yourself a woman."

He's been saying that ever since Amber walked out two years ago. Mickey has tried to fix me up several times, but it doesn't work, because I'm still not over Amber. We were together all through high school and university, plus my five year marriage. Maybe if I could figure out what made her leave, I'd be able to move on.

Today is sunny and bright, and I'm in a good mood as I stand looking down at the sparkling white city glinting in the sunlight. I'm happy because several sales were processed through my Ecommerce site during the night, enough that will guarantee a trip to my favourite ski resort come next January. Besides, a person just has to feel good on such a glorious morning. It is a day with no foreshadowing of an event which will change my world. I decide that a second cup of some exotic coffee is in order.

As I start to turn away from the breathtaking view of the city, there is a sudden flash of light which momentarily blinds me. Stunned, I blink, trying to regain my vision. When I can see again, I look toward the valley. My nightmare has come true. The city is gone. Trees remain standing, delineating the roadways, but the buildings have disappeared. I am shocked beyond belief.

Suddenly the air is filled with a humming noise and a strong wind swirls furiously, shaking leaves and plants and sending sand clouds in all directions. I hurry into the house. As I close the patio doors, I see a flash of red light twirling high in the sky. Before my eyes, a huge silver sphere emerges from the clouds and begins descending to where the city had once stood. The red light slows its spinning as the gigantic globe lands, flattening the trees. My dream has never progressed this far.

On legs that can barely hold me upright, I run to my computer to try connecting to the internet, but it won't start up which means the cable and telephone are dead as well.

Returning to the glass doors, I can see that several much smaller vehicles are emerging from the sphere. It seems they have no wheels, although from this distance, I can't be sure. The hovercrafts, if that's what they are, appear to be going on an exploratory mission. I watch in horror as I see them come up the hill, drawing ever closer toward my house.

I hurry to the living-room and peer through the window. One of the crafts has landed on the street just south of me. Four of my neighbours have come outside and are pointing at the vehicle. A door slides open on the craft and something steps out with its back to me. The sun is bouncing off a silver uniform and my terror is temporarily assuaged as I think this is a government spaceship manned by an astronaut. The neighbours approach the hovercraft and seem to be talking to the astronaut. He gestures to them to step inside and three of them enter.

Tom Bartlett shakes his head and starts to turn away. The visitor points something at Tom and a beam of red light shoots from his hand. Tom falls to the ground, writhing in agony. As Tom's body ceases to move, the stranger lifts him easily with one hand and throws him into the ship. His gaze sweeps around the houses and I swiftly draw back behind the curtains. He must have sensed my presence because he has turned and is starting up my drive.

Fear grips my heart. What should I do?

I run into the bathroom and lock the door, but my attempt at hiding is futile. Within moments I hear a heavy step in the hall. The bathroom door crashes open and I come face to face with ... the being. He looks human, but my relief is short-lived.

"It was stupid of you to try hiding from me," he hisses. "Come with me. Now."

I cannot move.

"You need convincing," he says, and points a narrow cylinder at me.

The pain is horrendous. I thought my whole body was on fire. Fortunately, I faint.

When I awake, I find myself in a hexagonal room full of naked people suspended horizontally in the air in small, bubble-like containers. Some are crying. Some are sleeping. The woman beside me is trying to cover her nakedness, but she seems unable to lift her arms.

My limbs are not shackled but when I reach out, my hand bumps into a clear, gelatinous, impenetrable mass, making any major movement impossible. Several people appear to be yelling, but their voices do not penetrate the gel and I can hear nothing.

As I look, five portholes open up in the walls and to my shock, insect-like faces peer in at us. Their large eyes are green and yellow, their scales a forest green peppered with warts or bumps of some kind. The nose appears to be a claw, with a menacing pincer on each side of it over the red slash which I assume to be a mouth. A dark green horn protrudes from each side of their heads and their arms end in a pointed claw with three fingers.

A door concealed in the sixth wall slides back and a human wearing white pants and a lab coat enters. After my encounter at the house, I fear it is more likely a pseudo-human. Behind him come six of the creatures which I now see have slim, beetle-like bodies. Their arms are large and scaly, as are their legs which end in feet reminiscent of a velociraptor.

The leader points to one of the bubble-wrapped humans. One of the creatures puts an arm around the bubble and carries the human out of the room. This happens four more times, accompanied by a lot of arm waving and what I assume is cheering from the creatures peering through the openings. When he comes close to me, I decide not to go without a protest. Unsure if he can hear through the gel, I yell, "What do you think you're doing? Let us out of here!"

He looks at me and smiles, if that's what you could call a gash that suddenly reveals a set of blood-red teeth. "All in good time." His voice sounds like a car scraping a brick wall.

"Why are we here? What do you want?"

"He asks what we want," he says, turning toward the windows. "Perhaps we should satisfy his curiosity and remove him to the dining-room." Unblinking eyes stare and several sets of grinning red teeth appear as the creatures cheer and wave their arms again. A blue liquid spills down their chins. I am quite sure I don't want to visit the dining-room.

"I think not," he says looking back at me. "He is young and strong and more suited for the fertility chamber. Allow me to introduce myself. I am Dr. Chana from the planet Nardra."

"How is it you speak English?"

"English? Oh yes. That is what you call your language. Those of us selected to be professional Nardrains have studied many communication methods."

"What do you want with us?"

"Well, you see a little problem has developed over time here on Nardra. Unfortunately, our species, while extremely brilliant, has one major flaw. We like the taste of each other much better than any other food we have encountered and there are those whose appetites are voracious and uncontrollable. Eating each other has caused the race to become nearly extinct. Given the gestation time of three of your years, naturally we can't produce enough offspring to satisfy our needs."

"Naturally," I say, as if it were the most common thing in the world to eat your offspring. "How come you, uh, people here aren't eating each other?"

"We are a select community of workers whose members originally vowed to refrain from eating each other. Those who refused to join or who fell off the table, so to speak, were returned to the store room."

"Store room?"

Dr. Chana lets out a sound like a full-blown car collision. "Forgive me. A little joke. It's the place where the - shall we say - less co-operative Nardrains were placed. On special occasions, we remove a few for dinner. The numbers are dwindling, of course, because they cannot refrain from eating each other. Those of us who made the pledge were eventually helped because our labs discovered a serum that diminishes our appetites. But we are all getting older now. That's why it's incumbent on us to speed up our recruiting program."

"Recruiting program?"

"My colleagues and I have come up with an answer to our dilemma. By inserting a combination of our DNA and a certain chemical compound into suitable humans, we can turn them into quasi-members of our species. From experiments, we have learned that these beings do not eat each other, which will help increase our numbers...a major step forward."

"You are turning humans into creatures like you so you can eat us?"

"Not exactly. Humans are quite tasty as they are. But just eating you would not solve the solution because, eventually, you would die out as well, or perhaps find a way to destroy us ... which, of course, is not acceptable." Red teeth grin at me. "No, our plan is to procreate using these genetically altered humans whose offspring will not eat each other."

"How do you know they won't?"

"We started our program several years ago. Through trial and error, we know it works." The doctor looked pleased.

"But you ... are you a made-over human?"

"No. I am a Nardrain by birth, but my current appearance is the result of early testing of the DNA, which, as you can see, was not entirely successful."

"I can see that all right."

"The successful cross-breeds and their progeny have been living on your planet for years."

"Impossible! Freaks like you would have been reported worldwide on the internet."

The Nardrain's face clouds over. "I suggest you dispense with terms like "freaks" unless you want to become supper tonight."

There were cheers from the windows.

Dr. Chana smiles his dreadful smile. "You see? There are some who would prefer to extend their lifespan rather than become someone else's dinner. Not admirable, but somewhat understandable."

"Perfectly understandable from my point of view."

"As to your comment about us being reported worldwide, that would never happen."

"Why not? You wouldn't exactly be inconspicuous, except perhaps on Halloween when all the freaky ... um, I mean when people wear all sorts of costumes."

"Perhaps I did not make myself clear. The alterations occur internally. The outward human appearance remains the same. You will still look like you to your friends. You will lead a normal life, meet some nice woman, and have children."

"But," my mind is boggling as I try to make sense of this whole nonsensical scheme. "If I have children, they will be pretty much human, right?"

"Only outwardly. Inside, they will always be Nardrains. The recombinant DNA contains one of our genes that can never become submissive. Once all the normal Nardrains are gone ..."

"Normal as in the ones who eat each other, I presume you mean."

"Exactly. As I was saying, the plan is to have the new species return here to live. Their lifespan is much longer than a normal human being. You should consider yourself privileged to be joining them. Given our high degree of intelligence, we will become a superior race that will eventually control the galaxy."

"This is ridiculous. I will not become part of your crazy scheme." I try to swing my arm, but the invisible shield will not give.

"Given your circumstances at the moment, I would say you have no choice." A blue eyelid descended in a slow blink and my bubble began filling with a purple mist which knocks me out.

I awake, totally disoriented, and find myself in my own bed. Was it all a dream? I look at my hands and feet. They are normal. I hurry to the patio doors and look out. The city is there. I have been hallucinating. Thank God.

Fortunately, Mickey is at home when I call. I start to tell him what a wild dream I had. He begins laughing.

"Have you been drinking?"

"No," I say, somewhat insulted.

"Then Buddy - I think it's finally happened. You've flipped your lid living in that empty house. Why don't you meet me at O'Reilly's. We'll tip a few and see if any aliens come in for a drink."

Although it is a little early in the day for drinking, I say I'll be there to celebrate being alive. Mickey laughs again.

O'Reilly's seems like a good choice. There are only a few customers in the pub and I decide to sit at the bar until Mickey arrives.

"Hi," says a soft voice at my shoulder.

I look around into the most beautiful blue eyes I have ever seen. The rest of her is gorgeous too. She is dressed in an off-the-shoulder white blouse and jeans.

"Do you mind if I sit down?"

"No. Please do." I am still in a euphoric state at finding myself in a normal world. "Can I buy you a drink?"

She leans toward me and smiles. "How very nice of you. Thank you."

"What would you like?" I smile back.

She does a double-take. "I, uh, I've changed my mind. I forgot I'm supposed to meet a friend.

"Wait," I call after her quickly retreating figure.

I suddenly wonder if my appearance is dishevelled, as I had hurried out of the house after calling Mickey. I go to the men's room and look in the mirror. My hair is a little messy, but not enough to scare off a good-looking woman. In my opinion, anyway.

I throw some water on my face and smooth down my hair.

"Much better," I say aloud and smile at my reflection, revealing a beautiful set of red teeth. I jerk backward in astonishment. Puzzled, I blink my eyes, move closer to the mirror and slowly smile again. My teeth are white. I was seeing things. Or was I?

Chapter 17

THEY'RE HERE!

Laura shivered. "Oh, I like that."

"Stuff and nonsense! Alien bullshit!" Colonel Montgomery said.

"You think so? I don't. I suspect there are aliens among us right now," said Derek.

"It's possible, I suppose," said Peter, "but I'm inclined to think they aren't on the planet yet. You certainly hear plenty about people who've seen space ships or UFO's."

The Colonel thumped the arm of his chair. "I think most of those people need their heads examined. Psychotic, the bunch of them!"

Leona groaned. "Oh here we go."

"But Colonel, surely you have to believe at least a few of them are as sane as you and I," Peter said.

"Sane?? Crackpots, I say."

"Well what about Roswell?"

He dismissed Roswell with a wave of his hand. "Another bunch of nonsense cooked up by conspiracy theorists."

"Not all of it. What about that Major who was involved in the original recovery operation? Ummm ... can't remember his name."

"You mean that idiot Marcel, who said the military covered up the recovery of an alien spacecraft? Phooey! And look what gave him the biggest coverage - The Enquirer. Can't believe anything printed in that rag."

"Oooh, you mean those stories aren't true?" Danielle said. "I thought those pararoozi always got the scoop on the real things that were happening."

"Pararoozi!" Angie giggled.

Dani raised an eyebrow and looked at Angie. "I thought everybody knew about the pararoozi ... those fellows who run around with cameras hiding in bushes. I know they're always following me."

Angie rolled her eyes.

"That's paparazzi, Dani," Carmen broke in.

"That's what I said."

"I heard there was also a mortician who claimed the government did autopsies on aliens," Peter said, not willing to back down.

"What you heard was a bunch of hysterical, misinformed people spreading stupid rumours. The government issued a couple of reports stating that dummies from a secret operation were recovered and mistaken for aliens. That's all there was to it," the Colonel said.

"As far as I'm concerned," Kelly said, "I think it's possible there are people or creatures on other planets, but as to the spaceships, I'll believe it when I see them."

"Very sensible girl," said Colonel Morrison. "You should listen to her, young man."

"I just might do that." Peter smiled at Kelly. "If she'll let me."

"I read an article the other day that said that a more than 2000 year old alien mummy was found in a pyramid in Egypt," Greg said. "There were several photos of it. The Egyptian Antiquities Department described it as a humanoid with reptilian traits that had been buried carefully and with honour. According to an inscription on the tomb, the being had been a counsellor whose name means 'Sent from Heaven.'" Greg paused. "An appropriate name for an alien from outer space, don't you think?" Without waiting for an answer, he continued. "There were objects in the tomb made of a synthetic type of material that no one could identify."

"Wow! Where did you read this, Greg?"

"On the internet, Kelly."

"Oh, and of course, there is never any misinformation on the internet," scoffed the Colonel.

Everyone chuckled.

“Of course there are things on the internet that aren’t true. What made this rather convincing were the photos,” Greg said defensively.

“Photoshop,” said Peter.

“Always possible, I suppose, but they didn’t look like it,” Greg said. “And all the experts who’ve seen it agree that it was not of earthly origin. Naturally, the Egyptians don’t want to believe that their amazing civilization might have been founded on the advice of aliens.”

Colonel Montgomery snorted. “More likely, they don’t want to look like idiots for believing such nonsense. But I’ve got a story that all you believers in this ghostly stuff will think is true. Nothing to do with alien bullshit.”

The Colonel took a big swallow of his drink. “Years ago, some of my army buddies and I were stationed in El Paso. We went into a local roadhouse for a few drinks and to try and cool off. Hot as merry hell out that way. There was an old fellow in there, quite talkative - I could hardly get a word in edgewise -“

A few of the guests exchanged looks and smiled.

“ - and he launched into a story, which he claimed was true, about a house in the town where he grew up Sounds better in his dialect, so I’ll do my best to copy his speech and tell it just like he told us,” said the Colonel.

Chapter 18

THE HOUSE ON DELANEY LANE

Ah reckon every town's got a haunted house. We got one right here in Summitville, for sure. Right at the end of Delaney Lane. Of course, there ain't no other houses on Delaney Lane so's you can't miss it if you go lookin'. None of the locals 'ud wanna go lookin'. They know better. Less'n it's some kids darin' each other. Kids've been doin' that for as long as ah kin remember.

Yessir, that old house has got quite a history. Ain't nobody lived in it since the Calhouns tried about seventy years or so ago. I was just a young'un then.

Of course, the whole dang business really started way back, about a hundred and fifty years or so. That's when the Delaneys lived there.

Maybelline Peckingham came from a rich family, more money than they knew what to do with. She was their only child and ugly as the misshapen sow what was born on King's farm last week. People figgered she'd never git married. No man wants to wake up in the morning sleepin' next to a face that would sour milk.

Matthew Delaney was, well, not exactly poor, but not rich neither - meanin' he was open to makin' some money, especially if he didn't have to work hard to get it. To everyone's surprise, he asked Maybelline to marry him and, of course, she agreed. Thar weren't no other boars waitin' in the barn to deflower her.

Maybelline's paw was a crafty old gent and word went round that he paid Matt Delaney to marry her. No one knew if that was true or not, but if yuh looked at Maybelline's face, yuh kinda figgered it likely was true. Probably was a pretty bundle too. On top of whatever money he gave Matt, the old man had a road cleared into a nice lot just outside of town, built them this big fancy house and the newlyweds moved in.

The Delaneys liked to host big parties, leastways Maybelline did for sure. Liked to act the lady of the manor. And, of course, people went to all the shindigs balls, I think they called them back then. People said Matt liked having all these parties, so's he could have some other faces to look at 'sides Maybelline's. Anyways, pretty near every couple of weeks there was some big 'do' goin' on there. Food and drink was plentiful, so people from all over the place was happy to attend. Strangers 'ud ask directions and folks started callin' the road to the house Delaney Lane, which was a might better than callin' it Ugly Lady Road, ah reckon.

You can well guess what happened. One of them destiny things. Matthew took a shine to some woman, or maybe a couple of them. People didn't really blame him, except for the other ugly old hens who was friends with Maybelline.

Anyways, Matthew Delaney started foolin' around on his wife. I guess he was pretty good at makin' up excuses for why he wasn't home.

At first he took his ladies to somewheres out of town. But then he musta got a little careless cause he made a mistake one night and some old busybody seed him and one of the women kissing right outside her door. Of course, she had to run right to Maybelline and tell her about it.

Well, Maybelline was some furious. Servants gossip and they spread the word that Maybelline was screamin' at them and smashin' things in the house. Matt took about a half a day of that and then decided to stay away till she cooled down.

Didn't work that way though. After a couple of days stewin' about it, Maybelline had got herself worked up good and proper, worse than before. Guess Matt's not comin' home was what sent her right out of her head and she decided she weren't gonna take no more.

Of course, Matt couldn't stay away forever and Maybelline took to sittin' up each night just a-waitin'.

Finally, late one night, Matt sneaked in the house. Didn't do him no good 'cause Maybelline was still up. She greeted him with several shotgun blasts. Killed him right dead at the foot of the stairs. Then she hung herself, off the top rail of the upstairs landin'. Nobody knows why, but they figgered she couldn't face the disgrace of what she done.

Next mornin', servants came in and found 'em. Musta been quite a sight, him lyin' there with his head half blowed off and her long skirts swingin' back and forth like she's a-fannin' him.

Nobody lived there for quite a while after that. Then an older couple from out of town bought it and moved in. Didn't last long though. They didn't say much about it 'cept to the preacher. He went out and blessed the place, but ah guess the blessings didn't work 'cause next thing we knew, the house was vacant again. Word got out among the townfolk that the house was haunted, but they kept it to themselves jest in case them spirits decided to start travellin' from house to house.

The place got sold a few times more but seemed like any time people moved in, they was back out in a hurry.

Like I was sayin', one year when I was young, the Calhouns came along. They was different from the Delaneys though. Both of them good-lookin' and charmin'. You could tell they was in love with each other by the way they was always holdin' hands and stuff, even in public. Us kids used to laugh at 'em, but they didn't care.

They had two little babies, a lot younger than me and my friends. Guess they wanted to raise the kids in the country. Sure did pick the wrong spot.

They spent a lot of money fixin' up the place. People were hoping that maybe all that paintin' and paperin' and workmen trampin' in and out might get rid of the ghosts of Maybelline and Matt. For a while, the Calhouns seemed like they was right happy, but it weren't too long before strange things started happenin'.

Of course, any local could've told the Calhouns they would, except for Swifty Sullivan, the real estate guy who sold 'em the house. Yep. Can't imagine old Swifty ever told 'em about the murder or the ghosts or anything else. All Swifty was ever interested in was money. Would of sold his mother for a buck if anyone had wanted her.

Well, like ah said, strange things started happenin'. First the usual stuff like doors openin' and closin' by theyselves, books fallin' off shelves, things disappearin' then showin' up somewheres else. That sorta thing. At first, the Calhouns were just a little puzzled, but as nobody was gettin' hurt, they just lived with it.

But then it got worse. Miz Calhoun started seein' spirits in the house. Not the drinkin' kind neither. The kind what floats down hallways and scares people.

Only reason ah knowed she saw 'em is cause she told old Doc Anderson, Loopy's Paw, and Loopy told me. Seems her nerves got shot to bits one night when this ghost with an ugly face jumped out at her from a closet. Miz Calhoun screamed up quite a storm.

Anyway, the Doc give her some kind of pill to quiet her nerves that worked for a while, but then things got even worse. She started gettin' forgetful and bad-tempered. The worst was her sleepwalkin'. Sometimes her husband would find her wanderin' down the road in her night clothes in the cold weather.

Got him real worried about her and them poor little babies what wasn't gettin' proper care from their mother any more.

Ended up he brung in a young girl name of Nancy McLelland from the village to stay with them and mind the children and help with the cookin' and takin' care of the babies. Biggest mistake he ever made, ah reckon. Rumour got around that Miz Calhoun didn't care for Nancy and was plain mean to her.

Nancy was a right pretty thing, and she and Bobby Hawkins was a-keepin' company, so she had it fixed to be off every Saturday night so they could go to whatever social event was goin' on.

In Summitville, most of the excitement on a Saturday night was if Swampy Barnes got himself drunk, and got into trouble, and that was pret' near every Saturday. One time he fell through Marshall's store front window. Damn near killed himself. Looked pretty funny though with his head restin' in amongst all the ladies' bonnets.

Of course, you could always count on Swampy bein' at the Presbyterian once-a-month church social trying' to get some of the local gals to dance with him. About the only one desperate enough was Prudence Wilson, an old maid who lived with her parents on Oak Street. People guessed she was likely near as ugly as poor old Maybelline Delaney, although weren't no pictures around to prove it.

One time, us kids saw old Prudence and Swampy kissing' out back of the church. Swampy heard us giggling' and chased Loopy, Chucky and me for a couple of blocks, till he got thirsty and had to stop for a swig out of the flask he always carried in his hip pocket.

Ah got off the rail there a bit thinkin' about Saturday nights. Well, like ah was sayin', Nancy and Bobby always went out Saturday night, and the night of the church social in April was when it happened.. Bobby got up and announced that him and Nancy was gonna git married come September. That gave everyone somethin' to talk about, so they was later than usual shut-in' down the dance. After that, Bobby took Nancy back to the Calhouns, leaving' her at the front door. That was the last time he saw her alive.

Nobody knew right away that somethin' was wrong, cause the servants always had Sunday off. It weren't till late in the day when Bobby went to Calhoun's to meet up with Nancy for their evening' stroll that he found 'em.

Bobby was surprised to find the front door open. He called Nancy from the door, but nobody answered, so he stepped inside. There, at the foot of the stairs was Mike Calhoun and some guy Bobby didn't know, both of 'em shot stony cold dead. Just when he thought it couldn't be any worse, Bobby looked up and there hangin' from the upper landing rail was his sweet Nancy, Miz Calhoun and some other woman, all of 'em just sayin' back and forth, back and forth over the dead men.

Bobby came running' back to town, screamin' like a madman, which, in a way, he was; least he went that way after. Sheriff Morgan hightailed it out to the Calhoun's, with nearly the whole village following'.

When he got there, he found Nancy and the Calhouns all right, and the two babies who were fine, but there weren't no sign of two other people, although Bobby kept insistent' there had been five bodies. Everybody nodded their heads. They all figured it was the Delaneys, cause we all knew they hung out there, so to speak.

Sheriff Morgan said it was obvious to him that poor Miz Calhoun had gone crazy and killed her husband and Nancy. The Sheriff's maw was there and she let go a piece of her mind at him. She said he knew as well as the rest of us that it was the Delaney woman's ghost what had taken over Miz Calhoun's body and made her kill those poor people. The Sheriff didn't argue much. He knew she was right.

That's about the last time anyone ever lived in the place, except for a couple of renters who only stayed a short while.

It's pretty run-down now. Swifty Jr., the real estate guy, calls it a "fixer-upper". Locals just call it the Delaney place.

Yes sir, we sure do have a haunted house here in Summitville. You can ask anybody and they'll tell you. Anybody, that is, except Swifty Sullivan, Jr. He's still trying' to sell it.

Chapter 19

GOSSIP

Greg applauded. "Nicely done, Thomas."

The military man cleared his throat. "Ahem. Thank you. Still don't believe in ghosts and all that stuff though. I only told this to be agreeable. Now I'm going outside for a smoke."

"Sounds like a good idea, sir. I'll join you if you don't mind a little company," Greg said, getting to his feet.

"Never object to company."

"This might be a good time for everyone to take a break. Please remember to help yourselves to the food back there," Derek said.

"A good idea. You must come and have something, Dani. You barely touched your supper," Carmen said. She adjusted her shawl and stood up.

"But I have to watch my waistline so everyone else will," Dani giggled.

"Getting sick won't do you any good. Come." She took Dani's arm.

"Very well. If you insist."

Leona approached Brent. "Have you given up smoking, Brent?"

"Yes, a while back. Too expensive and not good for your health."

"I was going to ask you to step outside with me, but ..." her voice trailed off as she watched Angie leave the room, closely followed by Derek. "Please excuse me, Brent," she said and marched out after them.

"Wait! I'll come with you," Brent said, hurrying to catch up.

Peter turned to Kelly. "I would love to see the portrait you painted of Derek."

She looked at Peter with sparkling eyes and smiled. "You really want to go to the library after Brent's story about the opera diva?"

"We'll ask her nicely to stay in her grave." Peter laughed and stood up.

Kelly joined in his laughter and took the hand that he extended to her. . "All right then."

Laura and Joe accepted drinks from the Pirate and drifted toward a window overlooking the back gardens.

They stood close together. "Any word?" Joe said quietly.

Laura turned her head toward him. "Not since the last call."

"Damn. I was hoping to hear something more." Joe sipped his drink.

"If we don't, then I think that midnight, or just prior, will be about right." Laura turned back to the gardens. She ducked up and down as if trying to see something.

"As long as everything's in place before the seance," Joe said. "I don't like uncertainty."

Laura straightened up. "Considering the unexpected plane delay, I think things are working out quite well. And I'm happy there was no reaction from Peter."

"Right. I didn't see any. That was a break. Of course, his mind has been on Kelly pretty much all evening. I don't think he'd notice if a wall fell down." Joe smiled.

"I tried not to make direct eye contact, just in case." She sighed.

"I don't think you need to worry. Like I said, he's on a one-track rail right now."

Laura turned back to face the room. "What do you think's going on with Angie and Leona?" she said, looking at Derek and Leona who had returned after a brief absence. The two seemed to be engaged in earnest conversation.

"He! No love lost between those two women. My best guess is Angie and Derek are having an affair. Too bad for her."

"Brent might be thinking that there's a divorce in his future."

"Little does he know that won't be necessary. Unless he and Angie are having other problems, of course," Joe said.

"True. I guess Leona loves Derek or she wouldn't be upset with Angie."

"Hmmm. Well, yeah. Maybe. I'm not so sure, though. I wonder if Leona had Derek sign a pre-nup. At least, she should have, seeing as he's a johnny-come-lately in the wealth department," Joe said.

"Right. According to the talkative Colonel during his rambles tonight, the family money was left to Derek's younger brother Colin, but when he died, Derek inherited quite a substantial amount. "

Joe opened his eyes wide. "Oh. I thought it was just the diamond strike that gave him money."

"No. Although he didn't inherit anything directly, he received the whole kit and caboodle after Colin was killed. You don't suppose ..." Laura looked out from under her hair.

Joe frowned and pulled his mouth sideways. "If the Colonel had mentioned that earlier, we could have looked into it as well. Too late now. Then again, having definite proof of one crime should be sufficient. So what happened to the secondhand inheritance?"

"Both he and Leona like to live in grand style, and the money was used up. Not Leona's, of course, because the Colonel is in charge of her trust fund, or something to do with her money. Maybe it's tied up so Derek couldn't touch it. Would have been a smart thing to do."

"Yeah. We know Thomas isn't stupid, that's for sure." He put his drink down on a table.

Laura nodded. "True. He's been a big help to us." She turned away from the window when she heard people returning. Angie's face was set in angry lines when she and a grim-looking Brent re-entered the room. Angie took a chair near the fireplace. Brent followed her.

"Oh," said Laura. "I think there's a disturbance in the force. Angie looks like she swallowed the sourest pickle in the world."

Joe's lips formed a circle. "Oooh ... you got that right." He smiled.

Peter and Kelly came back and headed toward Angie and Brent. Angie jumped up and left for the buffet table as they approached.

"Sorry. We didn't mean to interrupt," said Kelly, watching Angie's retreating back.

"You weren't. Did you two have a walk outside?"

"Actually, we didn't go outside. Kelly was showing me the portraits in the library. Some odd-looking characters there," said Peter.

"I think that has a lot to do with the era in which they were painted," Brent said. "For some reason, people seemed to think they shouldn't smile, or maybe they just couldn't keep a smile on their face long enough to have it painted in."

Peter looked at Kelly and took hold of her shoulder. "Kelly's painting is much nicer, of course. I think she's made Derek look younger and given him a sort of joie de vivre."

"You're being kind, Peter." Kelly blushed. "Derek was just in a good mood. I think he was quite proud to be getting his portrait hung up along side his ancestors."

"Did I hear my name?" Derek said, coming over.

"We were just talking about your portrait," Peter said.

"Oh. What did you think of it? I thought it was a very good likeness, although it's said that we really don't know what we look like because all we see is a reflection when we look in the mirror."

"I don't know much about art, but what I do know is, Kelly's very talented and did a fine job," Peter said.

"Absolutely. She did a wonderful job. I'm happy to have it hanging with the rest." He grabbed her hand and kissed it. "Thank you, my dear."

"Now both of you are embarrassing me," Kelly smiled.

"Ah, here comes Thomas and Greg. I guess it's time to get on with the stories," Derek said. "Friends, if you would like to take a seat, we'll start up the tale telling. Grab some food and a drink and settle in."

"I could take a turn now, if you like," said Kelly. "At least I would if I could make up my mind."

"About what?" Derek said.

"About which story to tell. I actually have two that I know. Neither one is very long."

"What are they about? We'll help you decide," said Peter.

"It's kind of funny because we were just looking at portraits and talking about them, and one of the stories is about a portrait. The other is, well, really creepy." Kelly shuddered.

"I vote we go with creepy," said Peter, giving two quick claps with his hands..

"I'd like to hear both," Dani said, fluffing her hair. "I'm always hoping to hear a story that has a part in it that I could play."

"I'm not sure you'd want to be in either of these," Kelly said, doubtfully.

"You never know just what might appeal to young Miss Dani," Greg Naples said.

Dani giggled. "Sometimes you talk like my father."

Greg grimaced. "I'm certainly old enough to be your father, I hate to say."

"So, which do you want?" Kelly asked. "I need a consensus. Portrait or creepy?"

"Come on, Kelly. Creep us out." Peter laughed.

"Okay," Kelly said. "It's called Feast Day. And just remember, you asked for it."

"WOW! Sounds creepy indeed. I have sealed our doom," Peter said, bowing to the room in general.

Chapter 20

FEAST DAY

In the darkest dark of the woods, where no man dares to tread, there is a small clearing where even the trees do not grow. Once every year, and always on All Hallows Eve, the forest creatures hide deep in their homes, not daring to venture forth lest they are never seen again. They know that on this night something evil will come to the woods.

A blinding flash of lightning rips apart a clear sky splitting the ground in the middle of the clearing. Up through the chasm from the bowels of the earth rises a large sarcophagus, which stands on a pedestal covered in grotesque faces. The door of the sarcophagus swings open revealing the horror of Radar, the Unholy One, who shakes herself awake from her long slumber. Banished forever from Kaldoma for her evil deeds, she is under a curse which allows her to awaken only on the day when spirits walk the earth.

Assuming her human form, she gracefully steps down from the sarcophagus and glances warily around with eyes that pierce the gloom of the still night. Pale fingers of moonlight caress her golden hair and light up a secret smile of anticipation as they pass over her full lips, softening her sharp features.

With ethereal grace, Radar swiftly makes her way through the woods, her footfalls barely disturbing the fallen leaves. No thorn or errant branch dares to touch her swirling gown or flowing hair. She stops by the ribbon of highway that splits the forest in half. She waits.

In a nearby town, Digger's Halloween party is in full swing. A river of booze has given rise to loud voices and laughter. One man does not look too happy, as he watches his girlfriend, Marnie, flirting with a couple of Digger's friends, one of whom has his arm resting lightly on her buttocks.

He goes over to the group and forcibly removes the tall man's hand.

"Hey! What's the matter, pal?" the man says, stepping back to look at Ned.

Ned's face is flushed. "I'm not your pal and keep your hand off my girl's ass," Ned replies.

"What's the matter, Neddy? Are you jealous?" Marnie says. She curls her lip.

"You're supposed to be my girlfriend and I don't like other guys pawing you."

"Is that right?" She leans back against the other man. "Well, guess what, Neddy ... I happen to like being touched by a real man."

Ned grabs her arm. "I'm a real man, and I'm sick of your constant flirting."

Marnie yanks away from him. "You don't own me, Ned Daniels, so leave me alone."

Ned takes hold of her arm again and tries to pull her away. "Let's go outside and talk for a minute."

Marnie struggles to get out of his grip. "Take your hands off me! Larry, make him let go."

"You heard her, pal. She wants to be left alone," says the tall man named Larry. He steps toward Ned and clenches his fists.

Ned assesses the situation. He has no intention of getting into a fight with anyone let alone a man who stands four inches over him.

"Fine," he says. "But don't come crawling to me tomorrow telling me it was all a mistake, Marnie. I've had it with your behaviour."

"Asshole!" Larry says to Ned's retreating back.

They all laugh as Ned ignores them and leaves the room.

He gets in his car and slams a fist on the steering wheel. What he expected to be a wonderful evening had turned out to be disastrous. He knows Marnie will try to come back but determines that she has made a fool of him for the last time.

As he drives home, Ned's foul mood lightens only slightly as he reminds himself that there are plenty of other women around who would be glad to have him in their lives. "I know you're out there. Come and get me!" he says aloud, looking up at the sky.

His headlights suddenly pick up a luminescent glow on the side of the road.

Automatically he slows down and peers into the gloom. A pale, frightened face flashes by. A woman!

Ned slams on the brakes, pulls over, jumps out of the car and hurries back to the woman who is sitting rocking back and forth.

"Miss, are you all right?" Ned's breath catches as she looks at him with huge green eyes sparkling with flecks of golden moonlight.

"I'm afraid I've hurt my ankle," Radar says with a sob as she hangs onto the ankle and continues to rock.

Ned squats. "I could take you to a hospital." He pushes her hair back from her face. It feels silky and he rubs it between his fingers. The smell of a rose garden in June fills his nostrils. He sighs, stands up and looks around. "Where is your car?"

"I wasn't driving. My boyfriend and I were supposed to be having a romantic evening under the stars, but we got into a fight and he left me out here. I fell when I ran after him."

Ned looks sympathetic, nods his head. "I'm sorry. Must be the night for relationships ending. Can you stand?"

"I'll try if you help me." Radar reaches up to him.

Ned puts his arms around her and inhales an intoxicating earthy perfume which hints of unspoken passion and heightens his senses so that her voluptuous breasts seem to burn through his shirt and into his flesh as she leans in to him. .

"I really don't think I can walk." Radar leans harder against his chest.

"I'll carry you to my car." Ned picks her up and she wraps her arms around his neck. He feels her warm breath on his cheek. He moves slowly to his car.

"Wait," Radar cries. "I've left my purse in the clearing. I should go back and get it. Do you think you can manage to carry me that far?"

"Of course," Ned says, happy to continue the close encounter. "Which way?"

"Through there. I'm sorry to be such a bother." Radar points to a small opening between two pine trees.

Ned smiles and assures her she is no bother. The narrow path forces Radar even closer to Ned and he feels a stirring in his groin.

"I'm sure I haven't seen you before. Do you live far from here?" he asks.

"Not very. I am so glad you happened along. I was terribly afraid in the dark." She opens her eyes wide and gazes at him adoringly.

Ned's breath quickens as he falls under her spell. Radar snuggles closer, leans her head on his shoulder. Her hair tickles his neck.

Her perfume is nearly overpowering now in its sexual overtones and Ned struggles to breathe. He manages to speak.

"It ... it's nothing. Glad to help a lady in distress, especially a beautiful one."

Radar draws back and looks into his eyes. "But you are my hero." She kisses him gently on the cheek just as they step into the clearing.

Ned is overwhelmed. It seems this gorgeous woman, who is obviously interested in him, has been sent to him in answer to his prayer.

He stops and gently sets her on the ground. Radar leans heavily against his chest and smiles as she feels him harden. She runs her hands up his arms and behind his head. She tips her mouth towards his and Ned accepts the invitation. They kiss and Ned is lost in the fire of their rising passions.

Radar steps back and drops her diaphanous gown; Ned gasps at the beauty of her form. He is totally under her spell and desire consumes him. The air is charged with the electricity of their rising emotions. She sinks to the ground, pulling Ned with her. Limbs entwine, mouths seek, hands search, tongues taste.

In the final moment of supreme ecstasy, Radar lets out an inhuman growl. Startled, Ned lifts his head and looks at her. Gone is the golden hair and soft skin. His eyes open wide in horror and he scrambles backwards away from the serpentine head with the gaping jaws.

The last thing he sees is a sword-like claw coming towards him. Without waiting for Ned's severed head to finish rolling away from his body, Radar tears his limbs asunder and sinks her green teeth into his warm flesh. Her blue-black scales glisten with drops of blood as she relishes each bite of her meal.

When nothing remains but the blood-soaked ground, Radar rises and retrieves Ned's head. She laughs at the terrified expression frozen on his face and his bulging eyes. She carries her trophy to the pedestal and jams Ned's frightened face into the base where he joins the others who give silent testimony to the feasting of previous years.

In the darkest dark of the woods in the clearing where even the trees do not grow, the moon moves across the sky and Radar takes her place once more inside the sarcophagus. Her belly is full and she is satisfied. The sarcophagus closes and sinks back into the ground. The forest breathes easier. Till next year.

Chapter 21

SAY WHAT?

"Whoa! That was creepy all right," Peter said.

"Oh my God. That nearly scared me to death," said Leona.

"Too bad it failed," Angie said. Brent lightly thumped her back and was rewarded with a dirty look.

"Ooooh ... I could certainly play the part of a gorgeous seductress. What do you think, Carmen?"

"There is no doubt about that, Dani, but I'm not sure how you would like having green teeth and a scaly body."

"They could always use one of those, um, whatchamacallit moving thingies you see in some movies."

Behind her hand, Laura said to Joe, "Geez, I'm sure Sound and Light would be thrilled to know they made 'watchamacallit moving thingies' for movies." She rolled her eyes.

Joe laughed.

“I think your story lived up to your description, Kelly. I doubt anyone will pick up a female in distress any more.” Derek laughed.

“Ye gads!” Colonel Montgomery interjected. “All this talk about aliens and now reptiles being found in a sarcophagus is enough to make Howard Carter roll over in his grave. You probably even think Abbott and Costello Meet the Mummy is true.”

“Abbott and Costello.” Dani looked thoughtful. “Were they explorers or those arcalegal people who go looking for old tombs?”

Angie laughed aloud. “It seems there is no limit to your ignorance, Dani.”

Dani looked offended. “Well, there’s nothing wrong with asking, is there?” She pouted and looked at Carmen.

Carmen glared at Angie. “Of course there isn’t,” she said, patting Dani’s arm. “It’s how we all learn. Abbott and Costello were a comedy team.”

“I saw several sarcophagi when I was in Egypt and none of them had aliens, reptiles or comedians in them,” the Colonel said emphatically.

“When were you in Egypt, Colonel?” Peter asked.

“Been there many times - last time was just before I went to Africa.”

Joe and Laura exchanged a quick glance. This was dangerous ground.

Peter’s eyes grew wide. “You were in Africa too?”

The Colonel puffed out his chest. "Yes, spent most of the last two years there in and around Dereleone."

"What's Dereleone?"

"The name that I gave to my diamond mine ... a combination of mine and Leona's names," Derek said.

Laura coughed. "Perhaps it would be a good time to tell another story. My turn, I believe."

"Good idea, Laura," Joe said. His stern look dared anyone to disagree.

The Colonel groaned. "Little green men running around, I suppose."

Laura laughed. "I promise you, Colonel, it has nothing to do with aliens or sarcophagi.

"Good." He settled back in his chair.

"It has to do with a rug."

The Colonel rolled his head and sighed. "Not a flying carpet, I hope," he said . "No Arabian nights or that sort of thing."

Laura laughed. "No Arabian nights, but ... well, you be the judge."

Chapter 22

THE RUG

The long fingers of the barren trees reached through the early morning mist scraping incessantly against the weather-beaten shed at the back of the property. Caught by an errant gust of wind, a shingle waved sadly from the roof of the small house. The elderly man working nearby was too absorbed in his own thoughts to notice.

Thwack! Another log split in two.

Dropping the axe, Rudy Taylor sat on the cutting stump and wiped his forehead with his sleeve. "Hot work," he muttered. A robin, picking through the remnants of the previous year's garden, glanced at him as Rudy rolled his neck and stretched his back to relieve his aching shoulders. "Not as young as I used to be. Time was I coulda chopped a whole cord without stopping. Like the year I won the championship at the county fair. Big, strong, handsome devil I was then."

"You sittin' down again, Rudy Taylor? Don't you know it's freezing in this house?" The robin flew off at the sound of Carrie's shrill voice.

The walls shook when the inside door slammed, causing several remaining flakes of paint to fall off the frame of the nearby window and a few of the clapboards that hung askew to applaud briefly.

Shit! He hadn't even had breakfast yet and already she was at him. He pulled a cigarette from the top of his ear, lit it and inhaled deeply. A man couldn't even take a rest without that bitch screaming at him.

Blowing out the smoke, Rudy thought about his youth. Handsome devil, I was then. Yes sir. Coulda had any girl I wanted. Course, Carrie was the prettiest with her auburn hair and green eyes. Never know it to look at her now, skinny and frazzled with a mouth that never stops yapping. Even talks to ghosts since she got into that spiritual religion crap. It was enough to make your skin crawl to listen to her talking to an empty room.

Her voice cut through his reverie. "What you still sittin' there for? No wonder it takes you so long to do anything. Not that you do much anyway. You ain't even started fillin' in that outhouse yet like I been askin' you to for weeks."

"Well, I could fill it in with you and your big yap," Rudy muttered under his breath.

"Laziest damn man God put on the face of this earth. Make sure your boots are clean before you come in." The door slammed a second time.

What a nag she'd turned into, whining and complaining all the time, like he never did anything. His sallow face drooped as he thought how she had changed over the years. Too bad they hadn't had any babies. Might have given her something else to think about besides him. Rudy sighed and thought of escaping to Rollie's bar, which reminded him of the bottle he had stashed in the lean-to. Maybe he could sneak a drink. But no, Carrie was likely watching him.

"Get your lazy-ass butt movin', Rudy. I ain't got all day to be waitin' for that wood."

Rudy looked up prepared to give her a piece of his mind. To his surprise, Carrie wasn't at the door. He shook his head. "Gawd-a-mighty! Am I hearin' her even when she ain't there? Things gettin' real bad if that's happenin'."

He threw the butt away. "Better get this damn wood in the house before she's really out here yellin' and hollerin' again."

The damp wind of late April blew several strands of overlong gray hair into Rudy's face. Balancing an armload of wood, he stepped carefully over the tilted board that used to be the first step before the nails came out. Struggling not to drop his burden, he tried to open the screen door with two fingers, but the lever would not give.

"Carrie," he yelled, kicking the lower panel of the door, "hurry and open this door, willya?" The door rattled for the second time under the impact of his big work boots.

"All right, all right. You don't have to knock the house down. Although that probably wouldn't take much," Carrie pushed open the door and a pungent wave of vinegar, rising from the newly-washed linoleum, escaped into the cold. She stepped back to allow his bulky frame to pass into the small kitchen. The flames of the kerosene lamp on the kitchen table, flickered as Rudy pushed by.

"If you'd fix that latch like you said, you'd be able to open it easier." Carrie banged the screen door three times before the perverse lever regained its hold on the catch.

Without speaking, Rudy made his way to the wood box where he dropped his load with a crash.

"My God, man, couldn't you be a little quieter? My eardrums is like to bust with that racket." Carrie moved closer. "And look at this! Bad enough the linoleum's already chipped so it hardly looks clean. Now you've gone and got wood chips all over the place."

Throwing some wood into the stove, Rudy only half-listened to the harangue continuing behind him. Like a broken record, Carrie always said the same thing over and over again. "Some handyman! Why can't you fix things around here, same as you do at other places. Just 'cause you don't get paid for doin' them here don't mean they shouldn't get done."

Her voice droned on and Rudy wondered why she didn't get tired listening to herself. He could recite the speech almost verbatim, having heard it daily since the mill closed five years ago. "Good thing she had that spiritualist meeting to go to once in a while," he thought. "Let's me escape to Rollie's."

When the wood caught, he slowly stood to his full height of 6'2" and, with a kick, closed the cast iron door.

"Make sure you get them boots off, unless you're plannin' on going back outside to take care of that outhouse. Which would be a real God's miracle."

Not glancing at his wife, Rudy removed his quilted vest, tossed it at the chair with the missing spindle, and lumbered into the living-room. The pale April light did nothing to enhance the few pieces of furniture which fought with each other for floor space. Even the reds of the Axminster rug were diminished in the gloom.

"What you doin' walkin' in there with yer boots on? I just told you to take them off. You better not be walkin' on my rug. You know I love that rug. How do you expect me to keep it lookin' good if you keep trampin' all over it?! Good-for-nothing man! I swear you're the devil sent to torture me!"

He bent over to pick up his cigarettes from the battered coffee table placed in front of the once-blue, now gray couch, whose worn patches were artfully concealed by antimacassars.

"There's a nail in the wall for this vest, ya know," Carrie's voice called after him. He knew she would hang up the vest for him; in fact, would probably be disappointed if he had done it himself. It had become the pattern of their life. He moved around, she walked behind, complaining about what he did or didn't do. She followed him now into the small, sparsely furnished living-room, dwarfed by Rudy's heavyset body.

"For Pete's sake, didn't you hear me tell you to take your boots off before you come in here. You're ruining my beautiful rug. I just swept it and you're makin' marks all over it!" Carrie went back into the kitchen, returning with a carpet sweeper.

Rudy moved to the window, brushing against the armchair whose faded red roses limped across the sagging back. Looking out at the dilapidated truck, he wondered if he had enough gas to get to town, far away from the bitch's nagging.

Behind him, he could hear Carrie cleaning whatever dirt he had managed to leave on her precious rug. She was always sweeping the damn thing like it was some kind of family heirloom worth a fortune instead of a second-hand rug that she bought at the church auction a year ago. You'd have thought it came from God himself just because high and mighty do-gooder Biddy Baggs had once walked on it. At least the bitch had used her own hoard of 'rainy day' money to buy it.

"Breakfast ready yet?" he said, still looking out the window.

"Of course it's not ready. How could I make anything without a fire? It'll be ready when I get to it. Could've got there sooner if I hadn't had to clean up after you. Why don't you go do something useful while you're waiting. That privy still needs lime put in it."

"Yah, yah. I'll get to it."

"Sure. That thing's gonna be stinking to high heaven before you 'get to it'. Too bad we ain't got any neighbors. If someone else complained, you might do something about it."

Tossing the cigarettes back on the table, Rudy watched Carrie as she used short, swift strokes to remove the last of the offending specks of mud. The tired lines in her pasty complexion were emphasized by the down-turned grim mouth, now pulled into a straight line of concentration. The loose print dress and oversize sweater added little bulk to her sparse body, and no trace of the vibrant auburn color was left in the grey hair pulled back from her face in a tight bun.

He waited until Carrie had finished sweeping, then with deliberate steps walked back across the rug, pushing past his wife, hoping he would leave more dirt behind him.

"You're trying to ruin my rug, you big lout," Carrie cried in dismay.

"I don't give a shit about your stupid rug. It's a piece of crap anyway. I'm goin' to town where I can get some peace and quiet."

As he reached the doorway, Carrie furiously shoved the carpet sweeper into the back of his heels. "You're mean and horrible!"

Rudy turned swiftly and yanked the sweeper handle from Carrie's grasp, throwing her off balance. "Who do you think you're swatting at? Too bad it ain't a damn flying carpet then you could get the hell away from me."

"I hate you, Rudy Taylor!"

"Good. I hate you too and your damn rug. Take this, you stupid bitch and leave me alone!" With considerable force, Rudy pushed the head of the sweeper hard against her chest. Carrie staggered and fell, the right side of her head striking the table with a sickening crunch. A slight moan escaped her lips as she tumbled in a heap face down on her prized rug.

Rudy remained motionless, suspended in the timeless gap which exists between action and reaction. He dropped the sweeper.

"Carrie," he called softly. Louder, "Carrie. Get up. You ain't foolin' me."

He nudged her body with his foot. A dark patch was forming on the rug. Squatting down, he tentatively touched her back. The slackness of her warm body astounded him. She had always been so stiff, so unbending. He put his fingers on her neck, but could feel nothing.

Ribbons of blood trickled onto the carpet from her head and mouth, turning the fibers into a grisly paintbrush. Sitting back on his heels, he looked at her lifeless form.

"My God," he breathed, "my God". Rudy stood up, barely breathing. "Shit! I didn't mean it. Not my fault. Not my fault. I'd better get somebody."

He stumbled to the kitchen. "No, wait a minute. What if they don't believe me? They might think I killed her. Shit! What if someone comes?"

He ran to the front door and looked out. Trees waved empty arms at him. The road and turnaround were deserted.

Back in the kitchen, Rudy flopped onto a chair and ran his icy fingers through his hair. "What'll I do? Gotta think. They'll never believe it was an accident. Never." Rudy's leg bounced up and down. "She probably told them we don't get along. Likely made things up. They'll think I killed her."

"Rudy. Rudy," Carrie's voice called softly.

Rudy jumped to his feet. He'd made a mistake. He was saved. She wasn't really dead.

He went back into the living-room. She hadn't moved. Gingerly he turned her over and placed his head on her chest. Suddenly, he had the feeling he was being watched. The hairs on the back of his neck began to rise and his body was seized with a great freezing numbness. Mustering his willpower, he slowly drew back to his kneeling position.

Terror mounting, his gaze moved slowly to her face. He saw Carrie's eyes fixed on him accusingly. With a strangled cry, he fell backwards, scrabbling away from the horrific sight, until he realized the eyes were as unseeing as glassy marbles. Gasping for air to feed his racing heart, Rudy sat staring at Carrie's body, until the shaking spasms stopped.

On unsteady legs, Rudy went back to the kitchen, his mind racing. He had to get rid of the body. But how? That was the question. Panic refused to let him think straight. "What can I do with her?"

He looked out the window. The frost wasn't out of the ground yet and too much work to dig a grave anyway. His glance rested on the axe, but he dismissed that idea quickly. Too messy. “Need a drink to calm my nerves.”

Rudy hurried to the lean-to and retrieved the whisky bottle from beneath a wooden crate. The liquid burned his throat. As he lowered the bottle, he caught sight of the six bags of lime standing in the corner. The perfect answer. She wanted that privy filled in, didn’t she? Well it was going to happen. Her and the damn rug should just about do it. There’d be nothing left but a few ashes and bone chips.

He started to replace the bottle when a sudden thought struck him. He gave a short laugh and walked back to the house carrying the bottle. He hesitated briefly at the door, then entered the kitchen holding the whiskey aloft in triumph.

“I can drink anywhere I please now. You hear that, Carrie? I’m setting this bottle on your checkered tablecloth. And I’m keeping my boots on, too.” A cold draft blew from somewhere. Rudy shivered.

He went into the living-room and wiped his feet on a corner of the rug. “How’d ya like that, Carrie? You and your precious rug ain’t gonna bother me no more. I got a fittin’ spot for both of ya. All I gotta figure is what to tell any nosy parkers who ask where you are.” Different ideas raced in his head. “I got it. You went to take care of a sick aunt. Sounds like a good story to me and somethin’ you’d be doin’ to impress your spooky friends.”

Once more, Rudy went to the front door and looked out. Although the likelihood of anyone being on their dead-end road this far from town was remote, he wanted to be sure.

Back in the living-room, he shoved the coffee table out of the way, and wrapped the rug around Carrie's lifeless form. He slung her over his shoulder, walked to the kitchen and opened the door a crack. Nothing but the damp air.

Rudy wrinkled his face at the stench that arose when he lifted the one-hole board. He threw Carrie's rug and its contents into the pit.

Taking pity on his aching back, Rudy carried the lime bags in one at a time. As he was about to fling the third bag on his shoulder, he heard a loud bang. A car door? Someone was here? The racing of his heart had nothing to do with carrying the lime. Panicked, he stepped out of the shed, in time to see Biddy Baggs coming around the corner of the house carrying a brown paper bag.

"Oh, there you are," she said.

His voice cracked on its way through his dry throat. "What do you want?"

Mrs. Baggs stood as tall as her 5 feet would permit. "I've come to see Carrie," she said indignantly.

"She ain't here."

"Lucky her," Biddy Bags muttered. Aloud she said, "Where is she? I brought her some special shampoo for the rug."

"She ain't here. Gone away to take care of her aunt what's sick."

"Oh. When will she be back?"

"Don't know. When the old lady's better, I guess."

“I see. Well, I’ll just go leave this cleaner on the kitchen table.”

Nosy Biddy Baggs in his house? Shit, can’t let that happen. Rudy charged across the intervening space towards Mrs. Baggs, causing her to back up a couple of steps.

“I’ll take it,” he said, grabbing the bag.

Suddenly realizing he might be acting suspiciously, Rudy tried to smile. “Uh, thanks, Mrs. Baggs. I’ll see that Carrie gets it when she comes home. She’s mighty fond of that rug, ya know.”

“Yes, I know.” Mrs. Baggs turned away.

“I sure am missin’ Carrie already,” he said, hoping he sounded sincere. “Lookin’ forward to her coming home,” he called after her retreating back.

Mrs. Baggs looked around. “I’m sure you are. She’s a fine woman.” Her feet made a hasty retreat toward her car.

“Yes, she is. Fine, indeed.’

As Mrs. Baggs was pulling out, Rudy waved the brown bag and called out, “Thanks again for the cleaner.”

He watched the car disappear down the road. “Bitch!”

His heart not totally back to normal, Rudy trudged back to the shed, picked up the last bag and took it to the outhouse. Trying not to breathe, he dumped the three bags of lime on top of the bundle. “Have a nice visit with your aunt.” He replaced the lid and returned to the house.

Rudy grabbed the whisky off the table and stomped into the bedroom, where he sat on the rumpled bed and drained the bottle. The alcohol quickly deadened his brain, and before long, his snores were the only sound in the quiet house.

Rudy slept all night, waking the next morning with a mouth full of fuzz and a head through which the hounds of hell were racing. Gripping his forehead, Rudy went to the kitchen sink and put his head under the pump, shuddering at the impact of the icy cold water. The towel dragged against his stubble as he dried his face. He wondered why he could not smell coffee brewing and why Carrie wasn't yapping at him for getting drunk. Then it hit him. Carrie was dead. He had buried her. He was free.

Rudy started the fire and made himself some coffee. He generously laced it with some of the contents of another bottle of whiskey he had rescued from its hiding-place under the steps. The scalding liquid seemed to drive out the last of the four-legged racers from his brain, and he began to practice just how he would tell the story of Carrie's disappearance. Then he remembered that he had already told Biddy Baggs where Carrie had gone. He knew he could count on her big mouth to spread the word.

Rudy drummed his fingers on the table as he mulled over the story. He frowned. "Oh hell. How'm I gonna say she got there if anyone asks? I almost forgot about that." His fingers tapped furiously as his brow wrinkled in concentration. "I got it. I took her in the truck over to Greensboro 'cause the bus connection was better. Right. Yeah. That's it then."

Satisfied, he got up, poured some more coffee and carried it and the whisky outside to the steps. The day was cloudy, but warmer. He sat down and patted his pockets. Empty. He had left his smokes inside.

Rudy jerked the door open and checked the kitchen and bedroom. He ambled to the living-room doorway and stopped cold.

"What ...?!"

The rug was once more in its place.

Rudy shivered. "Impossible! I threw lime on the damn thing, didn't I?" Then he began to doubt himself. Was I drunk? Somehow left the rug here? He moved further into the room. There was still blood on the rug but it looked different. Rudy leaned down ... and recoiled in fright, gasping for air as his heart began racing.

Scrawled in Carrie's blood were the words, "Rudy killed me".

"Who did this? Someone was watching." He looked around in terror. "Is someone here?"

Rudy backed out of the room. "Gotta think. Gotta think."

He hurried outside and collapsed on the steps, shivering in spite of the warm day and the heavy flannel shirt he wore. "It must of been the alcohol. I'm just seein' things, that's all." With shaking hands, he pulled out some matches, then, cursing, realized he had forgotten the cigarettes. Rudy reluctantly dragged himself to the living-room hoping the hallucinatory rug would be gone. It wasn't. Rudy grabbed the cigarettes off the coffee table and hurried back outside.

He sat down heavily, grabbed the whiskey and took several long pulls. Lighting a cigarette proved difficult, as his trembling fingers caused the match to dance from side to side.

Thoughts whirled through his mind like leaves on a windy October day. Had Biddy Baggs seen him? Was there someone else? But who? He was certain no one had seen him. The only logical explanation was that he had simply left the rug behind when he took Carrie to the outhouse. His mind latched onto that idea and a few more pulls of whiskey convinced him. That had to be it and now all he had to do was throw the rug on top of the lime and add another bag.

As he entered the kitchen, he caught sight of the cleaner that Mrs. Baggs had given him the day before. An idea came to him. "Just in case someone comes along, I'll get those damn words off there." Armed with a rag and the cleaner; Rudy went into the living-room, dumped half a bottle of fluid on the bloody writing and wiped vigorously with the rag. To his great relief, the words disappeared, leaving only a very slight pink stain.

After checking to make sure no one was in the vicinity or coming down the road, Rudy wasted no time in carrying the rug to the privy. He threw it in, along with another bag of lime. His stomach rumbled. After all his hard work, a trip to Rollie's seemed like a good idea.

Rollie saw him coming in. "Hey Rudy! What'll it be? Your usual?" He finished wiping the bar and threw the towel over his shoulder.

"Yeah, but I need some food with it. Got some bacon and eggs?"

Rollie smiled. "Sure. What's the matter? Carrie mad at ya?"

"Hell, no. She ain't mad. She's gone off to take care of a sick aunt. Probably gonna be gone a whiles."

"Oh. Too bad." He turned his head toward the kitchen and hollered, "Mickey, get a house special out here quick as ya can. We got a hungry man waitin'." He turned back to Rudy. "Feel free to come by for all your meals. I'll give you a special discount," Rollie said, smiling.

As his friends came in, Rudy nonchalantly related the story of Carrie's trip to visit a sick aunt. He was pleased that no one questioned him.

It was late in the day by the time Rudy drove home. The house seemed empty and very quiet. Just a little cautiously, Rudy looked in the living-room and sighed with relief. No rug. Taking one of the bottles he'd brought home with him, he trudged off to bed, dropped onto the bed and promptly fell asleep.

Rudy lay extra long in bed, planning how he would explain Carrie's prolonged absence. He finally decided to say quite simply that she had been killed in a car accident and was being buried where her aunt lived. "That oughtta do it. They'll even feel sorry for me. I'll stay inside for a couple of days while I'm attendin' the funeral." He chortled out loud.

That day, he went to town to do a couple of handyman jobs that had been requested a week ago. When he finished, he took his money and headed to Rollie's.

Mrs. Baggs was coming down the street, just as Rudy was about to go into the tavern.

"I'm sure Carrie wouldn't approve of you going into that establishment," she said looking down her nose at Rollie's window.

"No ma'am. Likely not. But then, I don't much like you poking your nose into my business either," Rudy said.

"Well! How rude!" Mrs. Baggs moved off in a huff.

Rudy laughed. "Stupid woman."

It was another late night and Rudy literally fell into bed. Visions of Carrie, the rug, Rollie's place and Biddy Baggs floated through his dreams. One of them kept calling him. He shook his head. The voice persisted. Sleep-dazed, he opened his eyes. Damn dreams! Then he heard the voice again, whispery, as if carried on a breeze from far away.

"Ruuuudy. Ruuuuudy. Come here, Ruuuudy." The voice was soft, coaxing.

Rudy sat up and rubbed his eyes. His head throbbed. "Who's there? What do you want?"

"Come here, Ruuuudy."

Groggily, he put his feet on the floor. The moonlight was strong enough for him to see his way to the kitchen. Rudy opened the door and peered into the darkness. "Anybody out there?"

No answer. He stepped outside. "Hello?

Rudy swore under his breath. "Must be the whiskey," he muttered. He moved to the top of the steps and relieved himself. As he closed the kitchen door, Rudy heard the voice again. Louder. From the living-room. He lit the kerosene lamp, blinking in the sudden brightness, and, on reluctant feet, went to the living-room, holding the lamp ahead of him.

The rug was back in place with the accusing words once more visible. Fear turned his blood to ice. Rudy began to shake. "I ... I don't ... understand. Is someone here? Carrie? Is it you? It was an accident. You know it was."

Rudy shook his head. "Shit! What am I doing? There ain't no one here. Carrie's dead. I'm just dreaming, that's what it is. Just dreamin'." A couple of steps into the room, his foot felt the carpet. It wasn't a dream. "I don't understand what's happenin'." His fright brought him to the brink of tears. "I didn't do nothin' wrong. It was an accident."

His fear gave way to anger. " It's this stupid rug, that's what it is. Damn thing was cursed by that Baggs woman. It's her fault. I know what I'll do. I'll burn the goddam thing." Furiously, Rudy dragged the rug to the woodstove. He fetched his hunting knife, hacked viciously at the woollen fibers and threw the small pieces into the fire.

"I'll fix ya. Goddam thing." The rug did not burn as quickly as Rudy would have liked, but at last, just a few charred remnants remained. He scooped the blackened fragments into the coal bucket, carried it to the outhouse and dumped it on top of the pile "That's the end of that."

His frenzy having abated with the burning of Carrie's rug, Rudy went back to bed and his trusty bottle. He slept uneasily that night, and rose early the next morning to check the outhouse. The black blotches were still there.

At Rollie's that evening, Rudy consumed slightly less than his usual quantity of liquor. Reluctant to go back to his house and chance losing another night's sleep, he asked Rollie if he could sleep on the couch in the back of the tavern. Rollie agreed.

Having slept through the night, Rudy awoke with a huge appetite and happily consumed Rollie's ham and egg breakfast special. Unable to come up with an excuse for remaining at the bar, Rudy drove home.

Very cautiously he opened the door and peered into the living-room. No rug. Rudy sighed with relief.

He decided to spend the night at home, and although his sleep was restless, Rudy woke in the morning to discover that the rug had not returned. He was so happy that he whistled as he drove off to do his handyman chores.

Toward mid-May, Rudy let word drop that Carrie had died in an accident. As he had anticipated, most of the people expressed their sympathy.

In early June, posters advertising the annual church bazaar sprang up all over town and on his way out of the grocery store, Rudy stopped to read one. *Won't be buying nothin' there this year.*

"Do you have something you'd like to donate to our church bazaar, Mr. Taylor?" a loud voice said behind him.

Rudy looked around. "No, Miz Baggs, I don't."

"Carrie bought my beautiful rug last year. I thought perhaps you'd like to donate it back. I'm sure it's just in your way."

"Not in my way at all," Rudy said, smiling.

"I see. Well, if you change your mind, you can drop it off at the auction."

"Sure. I'll think about it."

Rudy laughed aloud when he got in his truck. "Ain't that rich! The old bag wants me to donate the rug back." He laughed some more and wished he could share the joke with someone. "Yeah, right. I'll do that little thing."

Friday night before the bazaar, Rudy joined his friends at Rollie's. Most of them were complaining about their wives' plans to spend money the next day.

"You're lucky, Rudy. Ain't got no missus wantin' to go out there and spend yer money on other people's junk," Al Martin said.

"Yep, that's true. Last year, Carrie spent a bundle to buy old Biddy Baggs' rug. She was always yelling at me to keep my dirty boots off it. I hated that thing."

"So did you get rid of it?" Al said.

Puzzled, Rudy said quickly, "No. Why?"

"You said 'hated', like it was gone or sumthin."

"Oh. Well I meant I hated it when Carrie was yelling at me about it. Don't mind it now."

"Yah, well, we all hate the yellin'."

The men agreed.

On his way home, Rudy thought how he would have to be more careful in future. Couldn't afford to make too many slips like that.

Whiskey had become Rudy's constant nighttime companion. He found by drinking enough of it, the bad dreams had stayed away for months. That night, it seemed he had underestimated 'enough'. Distorted visions of disembodied heads disturbed his dream state. A voice called to him. Rudy tossed and turned, refusing to give in to the sound, but it persisted, until it seemed he could feel someone's breath on his ear. He sat up with a start, then reached for a bottle to control his spinning head.

"Ruuuuudy. Ruuuudy."

"No! This ain't happenin'. It's a dream."

"Ruuuuudy. Ruuuudy. Come. I want you."

"Shut up! You ain't real. Go away!"

"I'm here. Come and see, Ruuuuudy." It sounded like Carrie.

Rudy covered his ears. "GO AWAY!"

Silence.

He lowered his hands and once more reached for the bottle.

"I'm here, Ruuuuudy. Come and seeeeeee."

Rudy was furious. "I'll come and see all right, cause I'm gonna end it right now!"

He stepped into the living-room and stopped short as a pungent smell of lime and decaying flesh assaulted his nostrils. The rug was back with a new message glowing an ominous red: 'Rudy killed Carrie'. A luminous cloaked figure stood in its centre, looking at him.

"What the ..."

"Rudy, it's me. Carrie. Don't you recognize me?" The figure came closer. "Look." A skeleton hand with long, pointed nails pushed the hood back. Red light shining from empty eye sockets illuminated the globs of skin that hung from her face.

Rudy screamed.

The next day when Biddy Baggs arrived at the auction, she was pleased to find a note attached to a rolled up rug sitting centre stage. 'Decided to give you the rug after all.' She asked one of the helpers if Rudy had delivered the rug himself but was told the rug was already there when they arrived.

Several smaller items were auctioned off before Mrs. Baggs decided the timing was right for the rug.

She spoke clearly into the microphone. "Now ladies and gentlemen, I am very pleased to put up for auction a beautiful Axminster rug. This used to belong to me and I can attest to its good quality." She smiled and looked around. "And you all know I wouldn't have anything in my house that wasn't of the very best of its kind."

Mrs. Baggs' hands fluttered and a look of sadness crossed her face as she continued. "This item was purchased by my very good friend, our dear Carrie Taylor, last year and became her pride and joy. As you know, Carrie passed away just a few months ago." She paused, pulled a handkerchief from her ample bosom and dabbed the corner of each eye.

With a sniff, she proceeded. "No doubt poor Mr. Taylor was too forcibly reminded of her when he looked at it, so he has kindly donated it to be auctioned here today. I am sure you are all anxious to bid. If you three gentlemen will just unroll this beautiful Axminster rug and hold it up high so that everyone can see its fine quality...."

The three workers pulled hard on one side of the rug. Rudy Taylor's body rolled onto the stage, coming to rest against Mrs. Baggs' feet. Eyes stared unseeingly above long, bloody trails which ended in streamers of skin hanging at odd angles from his chin.

Women nearest the stage screamed, and a general gasp rose from the crowd. Biddy Baggs fainted.

That auction marked the end of the yearly affair, but that day is still talked about ... but always in hushed tones in case Carrie Taylor's ghost is listening.

Chapter 23

To Nag or Not to Nag

The Colonel snorted. “I might have known. More supernatural stuff and nonsense!”

Brent raised his eyebrows and looked sideways at the Colonel. “Remember, Colonel, “there are more things in heaven and earth, Horatio, than are dreamt of in your philosophy.”

“I didn’t know your name is Horatio, Colonel,” said Dani.

Kelly covered her mouth to smother a giggle.

“What are you talking about? My name is Thomas William Montgomery.”

“Mr. Richardson was quoting part of a speech by Hamlet, Dani. Horatio is a character in Shakespeare’s play, Hamlet,” Carmen said.

“Oooh! Shakespeare! I’ve never done any Shakespeare,” Dani said.

“What a surprise,” said Angie, rolling her eyes.

"I wouldn't mind though, as they have some great costumes. Is Hamlet a woman?"

Everyone but Dani developed a sudden coughing fit which caused them all to bend down, face to knees. It took a couple of minutes for everyone to recover from this sudden fit.

"At any rate, I liked the story. And Rudy got what he deserved," said Kelly, finally able to speak.

"I'm not so sure I agree with you, Kelly. Living with a nagging wife like that would be horrible," Derek said, giving his wife a sidelong glance.

"Women wouldn't have to nag if men did what they were supposed to do in the first place," Leona said.

"Nagging is not a nice trait and really doesn't work. It's much simpler just to go ahead and do it yourself," Greg said. "At least, I've always found that to be the case. And I've had three wives." He laughed.

Colonel Thomas snorted. "Well, the whole supernatural thing is hokum anyway. People don't come back from the dead."

"You think not, Colonel? I could cite many instances where spirits have come back to haunt a house or a person," said Carmen.

"And what about Mr. Richardson's story of the diva who wanted her headstone set upright?" Kelly said.

"Hallucinations," said Thomas William. "You'll never convince me otherwise."

"Speaking of ghosts and spirits, weren't you going to conduct a seance tonight, Carmen?" asked Joe.

"Indeed I am."

"We could get ready now, if you like," said Derek.

"But Peter hasn't told his story yet," said Laura, hurriedly.

"Oh right. Sorry about that, Peter. Would you like to do that now?"

"Sure. I don't know about the other stories, except perhaps Brent's, but mine is true. Not a ghost story, but more of a mystery."

"If you wouldn't mind waiting just a minute, Peter, I'd like to make a trip to the washroom."

"Of course, Laura. Go ahead. We still have plenty of food left, if anyone would care for something," Derek said.

"I think I'm absolutely stuffed," Kelly said. "The food has been just wonderful, Derek and Leona. And I've loved all the stories so far."

"Thank you, Kelly. I'll pass that along to the cook. I have to agree with you, too. I've also enjoyed the stories, so thanks to everyone for telling the great tales," Leona said.

"I'll get another drink before I start," said Derek, heading for the bar. "How about you, Kelly?"

"I'm fine, thanks."

"Anyone else?" Derek looked around the room.

"Scotch and water on the rocks please, if you don't mind," Greg said. He joined Derek and waited for his drink.

"Perhaps something to wet my whistle," Peter said.

Drinks were delivered and Greg and Derek resumed their seats.

"Sorry to keep everyone waiting," Laura said, hurrying to her chair.

"No problem. With drink in hand, I am now ready," said Peter.

Chapter 24

PETER'S STORY

"This story is something that happened in my family. Perhaps I should introduce the members before beginning. I have an older sister, Amy, whom I haven't seen for quite a while. She's a talented computer whiz and, as far as I know, she's still living in Chicago where she moved quite a long time ago.

"George is my older brother, a bit of an enigma. I think he fancied himself a modern-day Indiana Jones. Anyway, he left home just before Dad retired - said he was going to see the world. Have adventures. Something like that.

"I'm the youngest, a bit of a surprise, according to my Mom, Helen." He chuckled and then nodded toward Brent. "I recently came to Ottawa to work with Brent here, whom our family has known for many years. My specialty is civil action lawsuits.

"In between George and me, is Amy, my beautiful red-headed sister. My Dad, Mike, always said Any took after his Irish ancestors, a fiery clan who were always ready for a brawl.

"Mom had been a teacher, but retired to stay home and raise the kids. Dad ran a small appliance repair shop.

"Ten years ago, Mom and Dad won nearly four million on a lottery so Dad retired and they bought property up north in the back of beyond. There are about 500 acres, more than half of which is forest - very beautiful, especially in the Fall when it's a mass of blazing colour. They had a lovely log home built because they felt it would blend in nicely with the area. The only outdoor concession to modernity was the long, paved circular driveway. Dad reasoned correctly that it would be easier to plow in the winter.

"Within the acreage is a small lake containing a variety of fish. Dad is an enthusiastic fisherman and his own private lake was definitely his idea of heaven. He went fishing every day, including, we believe, the night he disappeared. But I'm getting ahead of myself.

"After buying the property and building the house, there was still plenty of money left over - enough to see them through their impending, so-called, golden years, except for one thing.

"Shortly after retiring, they took a trip to Vegas where Dad was bitten - badly, I'm sorry to say - by gambling fever. He lost quite a lot of money both on the tables and on the slots. Mom also donated money via the machines. At the time, the amount was insignificant considering they still had about half of the winnings left.

"The good thing was that there were no casinos near their country home, so Dad was able to avoid playing most of the time, but they still took a few trips in the warmer weather to places like Atlantic City, Detroit and Niagara Falls. Sometimes they won a little; most times, they lost. In addition, they took a couple of long cruises, staying in the most expensive suite. And, yes, cruise ships have casinos on them.

"I guess all of that added up to a lot and Mom confided to me that their money had dwindled to an amount that began to cause a little concern. She was worried about the money evaporating. Dad not so much. At least not at first.

"One day, about three years ago, George arrived on their doorstep. It was the first time he'd been back since Dad retired. According to Mom, George and Dad had many long conversations but she had no idea what about, and Dad refused to say when she asked him.

"I didn't see George because I was away at law school, but Mom told me about this later on.

"Just a couple of days after he arrived, George left again. Shortly after that, Mom was horrified to find that Dad had liquidated their Guaranteed Investments for close to a million dollars and that there was no sign of the money. When she asked Dad, he told her not to worry about it, he had things under control. And, true enough, at first, Dad seemed to be less worried about money than he had been before. As time passed, however, he became more agitated and during the winter spent nearly all of what remained of their savings at the casino trying to get a big hit. That didn't happen, of course.

"The following year, I came home for the weekend to help with the Spring cleanup. Dad seemed exceptionally happy that day, almost like the cat that got the cream. He said he was expecting some really good news, but that was all he would say. Mom mentioned it, too. She said he had seemed on edge for a few months, but had definitely been acting more like his usual self for the last couple of weeks and had been talking about them taking an extended cruise, perhaps even a world cruise.

"Saturday was a glorious spring day, warm and sunny. I spent the afternoon raking leaves, putting the dock in the water and launching the boat, after retrieving it from the boatyard service. Dad took the boat and his fishing rod out for a short while in the afternoon. He didn't catch anything, but said he would try later.

"Mom made one of her once-tasted, never-to-be-forgotten apple pies for dessert and we had a really pleasant dinner. I left the house about 7 o'clock to head for town and catch up with some of my local friends at our usual roadhouse. I came home about 1:30 am and found Mom in a terrible state. She said that shortly after I left, Dad decided to go out on the water for a while. When dark fell completely, Mom went out looking for him. She saw a light in the middle of the lake, figured it was Dad and that he would likely be coming in soon.

"About half an hour later, Mom thought she heard a loud voice in the boathouse. Dad was getting a little deaf and Mom decided he was talking to himself about something. She also heard what she called a "thud" and thought Dad had dropped something. When Dad didn't come into the house within a reasonable time, Mom grabbed a flashlight and went down to the boathouse to see if he was there. He wasn't. The boat was tied to the dock, but there was no sign of Dad. She called repeatedly, but there was no answer.

"I checked around. The car was in the garage, and everything seemed normal. Using my cell, I called 911, but despite my strong assertions otherwise, was told that it was too early to consider Dad a missing person. Too dark to do any more looking around outside, I sent Mom to bed with assurances that I would begin a thorough search at first light.

"A light dusting of snow had fallen during the night and the morning was damp and slightly misty. I put on one of Dad's old jackets and started off through the woods, calling loudly every few minutes and listening intently in between. It didn't take long for me to realize that I needed help to cover the whole acreage, although why Dad would have gone wandering in the middle of the night in the first place was a bafflement to me.

"When the Sheriff's office was finally convinced that Dad was missing, they formed a search party with dogs and volunteers. As the boat was tied to the dock, they assumed that Dad had returned from his fishing so that dragging the lake was unnecessary. Later, they changed their minds and conducted a frogman search all around the lake with no results. There was no sign of Dad anywhere and no sign of a struggle or anything at all to indicate anyone had been near the place recently.

"They continued searching for a couple more days, but then called it off, after deciding that Dad had just left of his own accord, but I never believed that for an instant. Remembering how happy he had been, waiting for whatever the good news was, I just couldn't think that he would run away. Besides, he loved Mom and ... well, just wouldn't do that.

"Mom had big posters made with Dad's photo on it and in big letters - MISSING - Michael (Mike) Morrison - and a note to call police with information. I think she had these distributed to almost every town in Ontario.

"The police wanted to talk to George, but we couldn't locate him, as no one had any idea of where he was. I don't know if he knows about Dad or not as we haven't heard from him in the last two years.

"After I returned to finish my semester at U of T, Amy went back to stay with Mom for a while. I guess his disappearance has become a 'cold case' by now, although Mom says Amy hired a private investigator last year to look into Dad's disappearance. There is still no information, as far as I know.

"Not knowing what happened is the worst thing of all. Mom wants to sell the property, but she's afraid to just in case Dad comes back there. I really wish we could find out what happened."

Chapter 25
REVELATIONS

Kelly touched his arm. "Oh, Peter. I am so sorry about your Dad. It must be horrible ... I mean the uncertainty of not knowing what happened."

Brent shook his head. "Very terrible indeed, Peter. How is your mother holding up?"

"She was a basket case for a while, Brent, but she puts on a good front. I know she's heartbroken though. She thinks he may be wandering around somewhere, not remembering who he is or where he lives. She's never stopped believing that he's alive somewhere."

"I think that's the way of the human heart. It never gives up hope," said Angie. She continued with a glance at Derek. "At least I don't."

"Some things you just have to accept as never going to happen," Leona said pointedly.

"It's been my experience that you can never be certain what might happen in the future. The best laid plans, etc." said the Colonel. "Things may be in play that you don't know about."

"You're right, Colonel," said Joe. "They say the only things sure are death and taxes. Personally, I believe the only sure thing is change. Whether for better or worse, you can always count on things to change."

"Carmen can tell you what's going to happen in the future, can't you?" Dani said, turning to her friend. "She's very good."

"I can tell you what will happen if you do certain things or continue doing something. If you choose an alternative to what you are doing, then the future will change, and I can tell you what it will be."

"Then I think we should get ready for the seance. Let's see what you can tell us, Carmen," said Derek.

"Um ... would you mind waiting just a few minutes, Derek," said Laura. "Nature calls. Sorry."

"Uh ... of course not," Derek said, looking puzzled.

"I'll join you, Laura," said Joe. "Er, that didn't come out right. I don't mean literally, of course." He laughed.

As they exited the room, Joe quietly said to Laura, "Quick thinking. Good girl."

"I will need a table," Carmen said, "big enough so we can all sit around it comfortably."

The Colonel coughed. "And I'll check it out to make sure you don't have any wires rigged up under it."

"Do whatever you wish. I do not need to use props. They are for charlatans and fakes ... which I am not. While you are setting up, I'll retire to the library to prepare myself."

"Brent, why don't you keep an eye on the table? I'm going to go along with Carmen to make sure she doesn't get up to any shenanigans?" said the Colonel. "And I'll check the table myself when we come back."

"Oh, uh, sure. I guess I can be a watchdog."

"I'll arrange for the table," Derek said. "Come along with me, Brent, so you can see it's a perfectly ordinary round table."

"Indeed."

"Dani, would you care to join me outside for a few minutes?" said Greg. "We can check to see if any witches are flying around on their brooms."

"Oooh, why not? As long as there are no bats. I hate bats!"

"Gee, it's going to look like King Arthur and his knights with the twelve of us sitting around a table," laughed Kelly.

"But they were all men. And you certainly aren't. I wonder if Guinevere ever sat at the table," said Peter.

"Unlikely. They may have been chivalrous, but they didn't let women sit in on siege plans or whatever they were talking about at the table."

"I'm not sure a woman would have wanted to hear their conversation, Kelly. Most likely bawdy and full of bedroom conquests. Then again, maybe they just wanted to eat food, belch and fart."

Kelly doubled over with laughter.

"Well, isn't that what men do when women aren't around?" Peter said between chuckles. "Oh yes, and watch sports."

"You are too much, Peter. Let's go catch up to Greg and Dani and find out if there's any Hollywood gossip to be had."

"All right. Or if I'm lucky, we won't find them and I can talk about taking you out for dinner some time soon."

Kelly smiled. "Will belching and farting be involved?"

"I promise not to do either - note to self: do not eat beans that day."

Leona watched the laughing couple leave. "Young love. Must be nice" she said wistfully.

"I daresay you can't remember that far back," said Angie. "Been a long time since your youth."

"You should know. We're almost the same age."

"Phooey! You are several years older than I, Leona."

"That may be, but I have something you want. Something, or actually, someone you're never going to have - at least not until I get my money. And I'm here to tell you, if you don't stop throwing yourself at my husband, I'm going to insist that you and Brent never come here again. Further, I'll make sure Derek stops doing business with Brent's law firm."

"What do I care? Brent doesn't need your paltry business. But Derek's not going to listen to you anyway. Face up to it. He doesn't love you any more, Leona. He loves me. He told me so."

Leona burst out laughing. "That's rich! You're a liar, Angie. Derek doesn't love you. Do you want to know how I know? It's because he's gay."

"WHAT??!!"

"It's true - not that he would ever admit it."

Angie laughed. "That's the most ridiculous thing I've ever heard."

"Oh really? Have you ever had sex with him?"

"I don't think that's any of your business."

It was Leona's turn to laugh. "I know he hasn't had sex with you because he hasn't had sex with me in months, er, years actually. I don't think he can get it up with a woman."

"I ... he ..."

"For that matter, I bet he hasn't even taken you out on a date."

Angie hesitated.

"I thought not."

"Only because we haven't had a chance. He told me you watch him like a hawk. We've just been waiting for the right opportunity."

Leona lit a cigarette. "Hogwash! I can tell you that 'opportunity' is never going to come. He's already had an affair with one man, and probably more that I don't know about."

"Well, if he's gay, which I still don't believe, why are you hanging on to him so tightly?"

"I like the prestige in the community. As long as he is discreet about his affairs, I can handle it. And more importantly - as I mentioned - because he owes me a bundle of money. I fronted a lot of money for his diamond drilling operation, and he's refusing to pay it back, even though they hit what looks like a never-ending supply of ore. Says he can't afford it yet. And there's no way on God's earth that I'm going to let him get away with that, not after everything he's put me through." She butted her half-smoked cigarette into a glass ashtray.

"I .. I don't know what to think."

"I'll tell you what to think. Forget Derek and concentrate on Brent. He's a wonderful man and you're lucky to have him."

"Brent's boring."

"And what do you think living with Derek is? Putting aside the fact that he's not interested in me - or any other woman - he spends weeks or months at a time over in South Africa."

"I'd go with him."

Leona laughed. "Oh, sure. I can see you now living among the dust, insects and snakes."

"Snakes??!!"

"Of course. They aren't mining in the middle of a city, you know. We're talking about the wilderness."

"Oh." Angie thought a minute. "Well, perhaps if he had love at home, he wouldn't go traipsing off to the mine."

"A long time ago, he could have had all the love he wanted right here," Leona said, "if he wanted it. Which he didn't, because, like I said, he prefers men. And that's fine by me."

"I still don't believe you."

"About what?" said Derek entering the room in time to hear the last remark.

"Leona's just been telling me that you're gay."

"What??" He flushed and looked incredulously at Leona. "Are you out of your mind?"

"I knew you wouldn't admit it."

"There's nothing wrong with being gay, but I'm heterosexual as you very well know."

"I figured she was lying," said Angie.

"I wouldn't lie about anything like that," Leona said smoothly. "But Derek would. He lies about lots of things. However, I have no intention of airing the family's dirty linen in front of other people." She nodded toward the returning guests.

Derek swallowed an angry retort. "We'll take this up later."

"Your butler has come up with a great table, Derek," said Brent. "And nothing out of the ordinary about it," he continued over his shoulder to the Colonel and Carmen following behind. "Guaranteed."

Servants carried in chairs and arranged them around the table.

"It pains me to say that I can attest to the fact that the lady did nothing except sit in a chair with her eyes closed. Waste of time, unless one is sleeping." The Colonel looked under the table.

"There is nothing wasted in meditating, Colonel. You should try it some time," said Carmen.

"Turning a bit of a nasty evening out there," said Greg. "Rain beginning to come down rather heavily."

"It seems to me it always rains on Halloween," said Peter. "Or snows. I remember once as a kid having to wear a snowsuit under my costume."

"You're right. I remember that, too," Kelly said.

"Now that everyone is back, you will please all take a seat around the table. It does not matter where you sit," Carmen said, "except for our host who will sit beside me."

"Of course. Delighted."

Leona seated herself on the other side of her husband and smiled smugly at Angie, now settling herself between Greg and Brent.

"And I'll sit on the other side of you, Carmen. I always like to be close to the source," Dani said.

Peter and Kelly sat next to Dani.

"You don't mind if I sit next to you, Kelly?" said Joe, as Laura took the chair on his other side.

"Of course not."

"Then I shall have the pleasure of sitting between two lovely ladies," said Greg, nodding to Laura and Angie.

Laura smiled and hoped he would not notice the cell phone on her lap.

Chapter 26

THE 13th GUEST

"I am ready to begin," Carmen said. "First though, Derek will you be so kind as to put out all the lights. There will be sufficient illumination from the firelight."

"Of course."

"Good. Now, I must ask you all to keep quiet. I need absolute silence. The spirits will not come if there is talking going on."

"I think we can all agree to co-operate on that point," said the Colonel.

Carmen arched her eyebrows at this unexpected source of agreeability. "Thank you. All join hands please." Carmen closed her eyes, inhaled deeply and exhaled noisily. She did this three times.

Kelly shivered and looked at Peter, who squeezed her hand and smiled.

Dani was sitting with her eyes closed and head back.

"We are sitting inside a circle of light to prevent us from the evil ones." Carmen sat quietly for a few moments, her head slumped forward onto her chest. The silence of the room was broken only by the crackling of the fire.

Carmen raised her head and began speaking. "I call upon the spirits who reside on the other side. Is there anyone who has a message for us?" She sat silently. "I feel a presence. Welcome. We are happy you have come to visit us. Do you have something to say to anyone here?" Carmen paused. "Very well."

Several moments went by. Guests looked at each other. Kelly felt like giggling but restrained herself.

"Is that it?" said Angie.

"Shhhhhhh," Dani hissed.

Carmen pulled her hand away from Dani and placed it on her chest. "I am told there are liars and deceitful hearts in this room. The spirit refuses to stay." She paused, then continued in a louder, frightened voice. "But wait! Another is coming! An angry spirit seeking vengeance for an evil deed. Beware!" Carmen's body shook and she cried out, "He is here!" She pointed at the doorway, where a shadowy figure appeared.

Kelly gasped and stared.

"Terrible spirit, why have you come? For whom are you looking?"

"I seek only one person. Deeerrrrek Beckworth."

"What!!???" Derek frowned.

"It is you I seek," the figure intoned. "You - Derek Beckworth"

"Oh really. And who are you?"

"I am your thirteenth guest, the one you did not expect."

"I get it. A Halloween prank." Derek looked expectantly around the table. "One of you set this up for fun. I give up. Who did it?"

The guests looked from one to the other, shaking their heads in turn.

The figure spoke. "You are looking in the wrong direction, Derek. It is I who have come back to obtain justice for my death."

"I don't know who you are, and I still think this is a prank." Derek looked at Leona.

"Was it a prank when you killed me two years ago?"

"Killed who? Who are you? I didn't kill anyone."

"Look at me, Derek. Surely you remember. You didn't want to pay what you owed. You are greedy, Derek."

"Enough's enough. What the hell's going on?!" Derek said, gripping the table .

"My spirit cannot rest until you have paid for your crime."

"This is ridiculous!"

"My soul needs revenge."

"I have no idea what you're talking about. Who are you? What the hell nonsense is this?" Derek said, his voice rising in anger.

"Look closely, Derek. Can you not see the man whose money you stole? The man you killed?" The spirit's pale face was momentarily illumined by the firelight.

Derek looked startled. "No, you don't look like any ..." His voice trailed away. "Michael? Mike Morrison?"

Peter's eyes opened wide.

"Indeed. You recognize me now, Derek."

"Can't be. You're dead."

"Exactly. But the dead can return, Derek, to seek justice. That's why I'm here."

"Is this somebody's idea of a sick joke?" Once more, Derek looked around the table.

"It's no joke, Derek. You took my life and now I've come to take yours."

Derek stood up. "I don't know what kind of hocus-pocus this is but I didn't kill anybody."

"You killed me, Derek. The guilt of it rests heavily on your soul."

"Bullshit! I didn't kill you."

Peter's head swung from one figure to the other.

"You know you did. Your last words were, 'You're history, Mike.' Remember? Then you knocked me out and then took my life with your gun."

"Prove it!"

"Look closely. Can you see the damage you did?" The figure moved forward.

Derek took a step back from the table. "I ... I don't ..."

"No? Let me come nearer." The slight figure came closer to the table and pointed to a dark spot in its temple. "You did this."

"I shot you in the chest not the ..." Derek's voice trailed off.

"Oh my God! DAD??!!" Peter looked from the spirit to Derek. "You killed my DAD?"

Leona gasped and clutched her chest.

Joe Walters jumped to his feet with a gun in his hand. "Don't move, Derek. You made a slip and we all heard you. You're heading to jail where you belong. Leona, turn on the lights."

Keeping her phone under the table, Laura hit a speed dial.

Derek swiftly hooked an arm around Carmen's neck. The chair tipped over as he dragged her to her feet.

Dani screamed.

Kelly's grip tightened on Peter's hand.

"I'm going nowhere," he said, "except out of here. Try and shoot me and you'll kill the bitch who caused all this trouble." Derek backed to an end table, opened the drawer and removed a gun. He put it to Carmen's head. "Drop your gun, Joe, or she gets it right now!"

Joe placed his gun on the table.

Derek headed toward the doorway, pulling Carmen along with him. "You - whoever or whatever you are - get out of my way."

The figure moved to one side.

"Give it up, Derek. You can't get away with this," Joe said.

"Not only can, but will."

"The police are on the way. You're trapped."

"Too late. I'm ..."

Suddenly, Carmen collapsed, throwing Derek momentarily off-balance. In that split second, the shadowy figure leaped at Derek, grabbed the gun, twisted his arm sideways and kneed Derek in the groin. Carmen rolled out of the way. As Derek doubled over, the figure gave him an uppercut to the jaw, knocking him flat on his back.

"Been wanting to do that for a long time, you son of a bitch!"

Laura picked up Joe's gun and aimed it at Derek. The Colonel hurried over and put a foot on the side of Derek's head while Joe pulled Derek's hands behind his back and snapped handcuffs firmly around his wrists.

Leona turned up the lights. She looked at her husband lying on the floor. "Asshole! I knew there was something wrong with you. I just didn't know what."

Angie looked horrified. "I can't believe it."

"You'll be lucky to have him out of your life, Leona. He's a bad one, all right," the Colonel said.

Dani rushed to Carmen, now being helped to her feet by Greg. "Are you all right?"

"Perfectly fine, Dani."

Derek looked up from the floor in time to see the 'spirit' slip the hood off his head.

"Son of a bitch! You!!" Derek dropped his head back to the floor and groaned.

The 'spirit' looked at him and grinned. "Surprise!"

Peter jumped to his feet. "George? Is that you?"

"In the flesh," George said, coming to give his brother a hug.

"Hey, don't forget me," Laura said, laughing at the look on Peter's face.

"What?"

"Is this better?" she said. She pulled off her glasses and the dark wig, setting loose a cascade of flaming red hair.

"Amy! How ... what ..."

"Just give me a hug, you two."

"How did your hair get so gray, George?" Peter said, pulling back to look at his brother..

George smiled. "Dye. It will wash out, so I'm told."

"And Amy ... why the wig and glasses?"

"We were afraid if you recognized me, Derek might figure something was going on. Besides, I enjoyed seeing if I could fool you, Peter."

They turned at the sound of heavy feet. Joe greeted the police who entered the room. Two of them got Derek to his feet and hustled him out the door.

"We'll need statements from all of you," one of the officers said. "I'll have someone set up … uh … "

"Officer, you can use the dining-room table," Leona said. "I'll show you where it is."

"Thank you. Meanwhile, Officer Wright will make sure you don't talk to each other."

Chapter 27

EXPLANATIONS

After the police left, everyone gathered together again in the living-room.

"I have so many questions," said Peter. "Who wants to enlighten me?"

"You're not the only one. I think we could all do with some enlightenment," Leona said.

The Colonel cleared his throat. "I would be happy to inform you of everything that has gone on."

Amy laughed. "No offence, Colonel, but you'd be giving us the Edith Bunker version and we'd be here all night. I think Joe could encapsulate it for us."

"Happy to oblige. You all heard Peter tell the story of his father's disappearance. What he didn't know was that I am the investigator Amy hired to see if I could find out what happened to her Dad, Michael. It's very often true that to find the solution to something, you have to follow the money. In this case, the money led to Derek, or more precisely, his mine. I discovered that he had spent all that he had trying to develop his mine in South Africa."

"You got that right. Plus he borrowed an enormous amount from me," Leona said.

The Colonel harumphed. "Against my advice."

"As luck would have it, George met Derek in one of the local watering holes and they became friends. He listened as Derek sang a song of financial woes just as, according to Derek, they were about to hit it big. He was right about the diamonds, of course, and telling the truth when he said he needed more money to acquire extra machinery. Derek said there would be a terrific return on all money so George decided to approach his father to see if he could interest him in investing in the mine."

"So that's where the big chunk of money went," Peter said.

"Exactly. My fault," George said. "But I knew Dad had gambled away a lot of his winnings, and I thought this would be a good way for him to recoup. Derek convinced me Dad's return would be nearly quadrupled."

"The problem was," George continued, "that after the huge vein was discovered, Derek didn't feel like honouring his commitments to the investors."

"For sure. I kept after him to give me back my money, with the profit that he promised, but Derek kept stalling," Leona said.

"And that's where I came in," said the Colonel. "I went to South Africa to see about Leona's money, and ran into Joe. We actually met quite by accident. One night - it was one of those hot, muggy nights and the locals were ..."

Amy broke in. "Colonel, we promised to keep it short."

The Colonel sniffed. "Very well."

"Shortly after the strike, I phoned Dad and told him he would be getting his money very soon," George said.

"That's why Mom noticed that he was much happier."

"Right, Peter. Little did I know that Derek had other ideas. Unknown to me, he contacted Dad and arranged to meet him supposedly to give him a cheque. Instead, he knocked him out - that was the thud Mom heard - and carried him away, most likely to where he had parked his car - a rental - just a short distance away and not visible from the house . I have Dad's build, so you can see it would be no problem for a man Derek's size to carry a 160 lb. man."

"He couldn't risk shooting your Dad in the boathouse, as even silencers don't render a gun silent," Joe added. "And unless Derek tells us, we may never know where he put Michael's body."

"Peter, I am so, so sorry. And you, too, George. What a terrible thing to have happen." Kelly touched each of them on the arm.

"How did you discover that he went to visit your home?" Greg asked.

"Let me answer that," Joe said. "After many inquiries, I found out that Derek had chartered a private plane on the day that Michael went missing. What made that difficult to discover was that he had driven to a small airport outside Oshawa to get the plane. The flight from there was less than two hours. He arrived home in the middle of the night, not an unusual occurrence."

"That's true. I wouldn't have known, as we have separate bedrooms," Leona said, looking pointedly at Angie.

"I think I understand the why and the how of what happened," said Peter, "but I'm not sure where you came up with the idea of making him admit his guilt."

"My turn," said Amy/Laura. "Joe and I really do work together. The Colonel again was very helpful. We knew we had to trick Derek somehow because although there was motive and opportunity, everything we had was really circumstantial. The Colonel mentioned tonight's party and that a psychic would be here. I suggested a seance during which George, looking like Dad, would make an appearance. The Colonel contacted Carmen who graciously agreed to go along with our scheme, and for that, we owe her a huge thanks."

"Indeed. Thank you so much, Carmen," said Peter.

"But, Colonel, I thought you said all this psychic stuff was nonsense."

"All part of the act, Kelly."

"Carmen, was your falling part of the ruse?" said Peter.

"No. Because we didn't know Derek was going to grab me. I just thought if I sagged my weight against him, somebody might be able to do something to stop him from escaping."

"That was very quick thinking on your part, Carmen."

"Thank you, Amy."

"I think you were absolutely wonderful, Carmen. I'm sure I would have just fainted dead away if Derek had grabbed me like that. It might be interesting to play a scene like that though. If I ever get the opportunity, I'll remember what you did."

"No doubt, you would do a fabulous acting job, Dani."

"I think that about wraps up all of our adventures," said Joe. "Amy or George, do you have anything you want to add?"

They shook their heads.

"Ahem. I might like to add a few words," Colonel Thomas said.

Leona barely restrained a groan.

"All I want to say is that it was a pleasure working with you, Joe, Amy and George. Gave this old man something to think about besides approaching old age. If you should ever need help again, just give me a call. And, Leona, we'll have to get together with Brent and see what we can do about your money."

Joe approached the Colonel and extended his hand. "Thomas, it was very nice working with you, and we are all extremely grateful for your help."

"Agreed," said Amy.

Chapter 28

FAREWELLS

"Joe, I have a question."

"What, Peter?"

"You and Amy ... are you, uh, business partners, and if so, what happened to the graphics job, Amy, and that fellow, Nick something or other?"

Amy laughed. "I guess it has been a while since we talked. Nick and I split up way back when. I took a law enforcement course that Joe was teaching and ... let's just say Joe and I are not only partners in crime, or the solving of it, but we're getting married next Spring."

"Oh, how perfectly wonderful! I hope we're all invited," Dani exclaimed. "Unless, of course, I'm shooting at the time. Uh, a movie that is, not people." Dani giggled.

"You'd be most welcome," Amy said, imagining how her friends' eyes would pop if Dani Davis came walking in.

"I think I've had enough excitement for one night," said Greg. "What about you, Carmen, Dani? Ready to call it a night?"

Carmen rose. "I am exhausted. It has been a pleasure meeting all of you."

"Absolutely wonderful. And I am SO looking forward to your wedding, Amy. Ta ta everyone." Amy wiggled her fingers as she left the room, immediately followed by Carmen and Greg.

Greg turned and looked back at the room. "I must say this has been a far more entertaining evening than any I've attended in Hollywood." He smiled and nodded his head. "Goodnight, everyone."

"I'll see you to the door." Leona linked her arm in Greg's.

"Well, I'm off to my room," said Thomas. "Safe trip all of you. And keep in touch."

"You ready to go home now, Angie?"

A very subdued and apparently sober Angie nodded and rose to her feet.

"Goodnight everyone," Brent said.

Angie nodded to the group and walked across the room. They arrived there just as Leona returned.

"It's been quite an evening, Leona. We'll schedule a meeting sometime later in the week. Do you want me to get a lawyer for Derek so he could try and arrange bail?"

Leona threw her head back and laughed. "You're kidding, right? He can rot in jail for the rest of his life as far as I'm concerned. You're not going to be his lawyer, are you?"

"Not if you want me to help get your finances straightened out. It would be a conflict of interest."

"Good. Then forget about helping that weasel. He's where he belongs."

"As you wish."

"Leona, I ... I'm, uh, sorry for what happened," Angie said.

"Unhunh. Can't blame you. He deceived a lot of people. Just remember the advice I gave you, Angie." She nodded her head toward Brent. "You've got a good one. Keep him happy."

"True. But I just have to know. Is Derek really gay?"

Leona laughed nastily. "I guess we'll find out when he goes to jail, won't we." She laughed again.

"Oh."

"What was that all about," said Derek, as they were exiting the room.

"Nothing. Let's go."

"Leona, we'll be getting out of your hair too," Joe said, tucking Amy's arm in his..

"Did you want us to call a doctor or anyone for you? You've had quite a bit of a shock this evening," Amy said.

Leona smiled. "Thanks for offering, but not as much of a shock as you might think. I'm fine."

"Kelly, can I give you a ride home?" said Peter.

"Why I, uh ... yes. That would be great."

"Hang on, bro. Can you put me up for tonight? My plane was late getting in and I don't have a reservation anywhere."

"Sure. Here." Peter handed George a set of keys.

George looked at the keys and then at Peter. "Ummm, I need a lift too. Would you mind dropping me off there as well?"

Peter's mouth opened slightly and he stared at his brother. "You want to ride with Kelly and me?"

"Of course. Call it big brother's revenge for all those times you interfered in my dates."

They all laughed.

"Okay, but you get dropped off first," Peter said.

The brothers high-fived. "Deal."

"See what you're getting yourself into," Amy said, laughing as she leaned against Joe.

"I think I can handle it," Joe replied, putting his arm around her. "Better call us a cab. I don't think Peter wants any more company."

"Oh, I don't know. I'm sure we could squeeze in somewhere," Amy said, "right, Peter?"

Peter rolled his eyes at her, then turned to Leona. "Good-night, Leona. I hope things work out for you."

"Thanks, Peter. I may run into you when I come to see Brent next week."

"Looking forward to that."

"Bye," said Kelly.

Leona stood watching the five of them happily talking on the walkway as they waited for their vehicles. A sudden sadness enveloped her. They were so young. The smile she had been forcing gave way to the tears that had been threatening.

"I hope they have better luck than I did," she said. As Leona turned to go back in the house, she ran right into the skeleton still hanging in the doorway. "Damn thing!" Angrily, she yanked the dancing bones off the hook and went inside. Leona sighed. "Well, life goes on - except for you, you bag of bones," she said, tossing the hated skeleton across the hall.

THE END

Thank you for purchasing The 13th Guest. For your additional enjoyment, I am including the following bonus material.

OPPORTUNITY KNOCKS

TARA

OPPORTUNITY KNOCKS

© 2016 Ruth S. Daigneault

"There it goes!" Scott Harris yelled, as the mouse disappeared behind the couch.

As befits a queen, Miss Tibbles ignored this outburst and continued grooming herself.

He glowered at the feline. "Damn cat. I don't know why Mollie didn't take you when she left. Oh, wait a minute. Yes, I do. You're a lazy, good-for-nothing creature who eats and sleeps all day."

On cue, Miss Tibbles stretched out languorously in a sunny spot on the carpet and promptly went to sleep.

The phone rang. Scott punched 'Talk' and grouched a "hello".

"Obviously still the sweet and loveable man I left," Mollie said. "What's the matter with you?"

"I've got a mouse problem and a stupid cat - the only thing you left behind - who isn't doing anything about it."

"Miss Tibbles was your idea, not mine."

Scott rolled his eyes. "What do you want, Mollie?"

"My support cheque didn't arrive and ..."

"Give me a break, willya? I'm trying to sell the house and I've got bills to pay."

"Well, so do I. And I need the money you promised me. Why don't you ask your bimbo to help you out?"

Scott gritted his teeth. "Joanne is not a bimbo and she's certainly not mine, like I told you before. Let's leave her out of this. Have you been to a lawyer yet?"

"No. There's no rush as long as you pay me the money we agreed on."

"I'll get the money to you as soon as I can."

"That better be REAL soon, Scott. I don't enjoy these conversations." The line went dead.

Scott banged the phone down. Miss Tibbles opened one eye, then went back to sleep.

With a groan, Scott threw himself down on the couch. "How the hell did I get into this mess?" he asked. The answer in his head, wherever it came from, was always the same. *Because you did something stupid.*

"Yeah, yeah, yeah," he said aloud. "I did a couple of stupid things, not the least of which was marrying Mollie in the first place. I should have realized all she really wanted was to get as much as she could out of me. And taking my secretary to lunch to celebrate her engagement was dumb too." Scott sat staring idly into space. Out of the corner of his eye, he saw the mouse peek out from behind the couch and scurry across the floor past Miss Tibbles, who slept on peacefully.

The phone rang again. Scott grabbed it. "I told you I'd get the money to you as soon as I could," he shouted.

"Uh, hold on, buddy. You don't owe me any money, although if you happen to be really flush, you can toss a few my way."

"Aw, geez, Glen ... sorry. I thought it was Mollie calling back."

"Bad day, huh? Then I have a perfect idea. Why don't we go throw a few back at Petey's?"

"I don't think I'd be very good company, Glen."

"And you think there have never been other times in the last year or so that I've known you where you haven't been good company?"

Glen laughed. "Anyway, that's what friends are for ... the good times and the bad. So how about it? Take a cab and I'll meet you in twenty minutes. It'll do you good to get out of the house."

Scott thought it over and finally agreed, but said he would ride his bicycle. Maybe Glen was right. He did need to get away from the bad memories.

As Scott entered Petey's Bar and Grill, he saw Glen sitting at the bar. It was hard to miss Glen Murray in any crowd. He was tall, muscular and his golden blonde hair shone like a beacon even in the dim light of the crowded room. Glen spotted Scott and waved him over to the empty stool on his right.

"A couple of beers over here," Glen called to the bartender. "So," he said, turning to Scott. "Is Mollie giving you a hard time?"

"You could say that. She's always harassing me about money. Drives me crazy. Phone call after phone call."

"Why don't you get to a lawyer, pal, and get this thing settled?"

"Frankly, I haven't got all the money for a retainer yet. Should have soon though. And, of course, if the house sells, that will really help, although Green Hills real estate isn't moving much right now."

Scott finished his beer and ordered another while he watched Glen surveying the room. Glen was always on the lookout for the greatest woman in the world. Amazingly, he must have found more than three dozen of them that Scott knew about. Scott smiled to himself. Glen would never change. Always on the prowl, always taking advantage when he could. A real opportunist.

"See that blonde over there?" Glen said. "She's gorgeous."

"Her hair's the same colour as yours. Are you sure she's not a long-lost twin?"

Glen laughed. "Nope. They broke the mold after I was born." He leaned back against the bar. "I think she's giving me the eye. Gotta take advantage when opportunity knocks. Do you mind, buddy?"

"Sure, go ahead. Oh, before I forget, I changed the phone number after I talked to you. It's 555-5543. Wait a second. I'll write it down," Scott said, reaching for a napkin.

"Okay. Keep in touch, Scott." Glen tossed some bills on the counter and picked up the napkin. "My treat. Wish me luck."

Scott watched his friend head off to the next greatest woman in the world and idly wondered how long this one would last. As far as he could recall, the record was two months. Before Scott finished his beer, Glen and the woman left. Scott looked at the football game in progress on the TV above the bar and decided another beer was definitely in order.

"What's the score?" said the man next to Scott.

"Not sure," Scott said, taking a quick glance at the man.

The man sighed and pushed up his rimless glasses into the lank brown hair that hung low over his forehead. "Doesn't matter. I'm too pissed off to care."

Scott turned toward the man. He took in the suit, shirt collar unbuttoned, tie askew and pegged him as a disillusioned businessman. "Me too. What's your problem?"

"My wife. Ex-wife I should say. Or she soon will be."

"I know what you mean. My almost-ex is giving me a hard time too," Scott said.

"Women are the root of all men's problems, in my opinion." He shoved his glasses higher. "My name's Bob." He extended his hand.

"Scott. Brings that old saw to mind, Bob. You can't live with them or without them, in some cases, I guess."

"Certainly true about my wife, for sure. All she really wants is money." Bob sighed. "She got the house and still wants more. The support payments are killing me."

Scott broadened the puddle of water with the bottom side of his beer bottle. "Really? Sounds like mine. Maybe they're related."

Bob tipped his head back, shut his eyes momentarily. "I think there's something we should be able to do about it, don't you?"

Scott raised his eyebrows and tilted his head sideways. "Well, nothing I can think of that wouldn't land me in jail."

Bob lowered his head and looked directly at Scott. "I think we could avoid that with a good plan."

Scott tossed off the rest of his beer and rose. "Let me know if you think of one. Have a good night."

"I will. You too."

Scott unlocked his bike and pedalled home, enjoying the slightly cool evening air.

Miss Tibbles met him at the door, meowed plaintively and wound around his legs, leaving a trail of orange and white fur on his pants.

He looked down at the cat. "Let me guess. You're out of food. That's the only time I get an official greeting."

Miss Tibbles led the way to the kitchen and Scott opened a can of cat food. "God, this stuff stinks," he said aloud.

He left Miss Tibbles to enjoy her meal, pushed the Keurig and took a coffee into the living-room to watch the nightly news.

The phone rang. Scott groaned. *Mollie!* Then he realized that Mollie couldn't possibly have his new number and that it must be Glen.

"Yeah, bro, what's up?"

There was a slight hesitation on the other end. "Scott?"

"Yes." Scott frowned. "Who's this?"

"Bob. We met in the bar tonight."

"Who? Oh, yeah. How did you get this number?"

"I overheard you telling your friend. I have a proposition for you."

"If it involves money, I don't have any."

"I gathered that. But this is a proposition to save you money."

"Are you one of these get-rich-quick scammers?"

Bob chuckled. "No, not at all. You'll recall that I said it was possible to stop our almost-exes from bleeding us dry? I have a proposal that will let you keep all the money from the sale of your house, without having to give anything to your wife."

"I see. Are you a lawyer or something?"

"No, I'm just a man like you. We both have the same problem and I can do something for you and you can return the favour."

"Return the favour? Hmmm." Scott frowned.

"At least listen to my plan. You see, I understand your situation perfectly. I'm in the same position myself, like I told you. My wife is going to divorce me and take everything I've worked for. I don't want to see that happen and I'm sure you don't either."

"And ..."

"If they weren't around, we wouldn't have to pay them, would we?"

Scott grew uncomfortable. "Uh ... exactly what do you mean?"

"We both want to get rid of our wives, so we help each other out. Like I said, return the favour."

"Oh, wait a minute," Scott said. "I've seen Strangers on a Train. Are you about to suggest that I murder your wife and you'll do the same to mine?"

"I prefer to think of it as eliminating our mutual problems."

"You're crazy, mister. I'm not about to kill anyone. This conversation is over." Scott hung up the phone.

Sleep did not come easy to Scott that night. Vivid dreams of Mollie floating in pools of blood haunted him. He was awakened from his dreams by the ringing of the telephone. At the foot of the bed, Miss Tibbles looked annoyed at this disturbance. Scott peered at the clock. 2 a.m. "Hello?"

"Scott!!! Great news!"

"Geez, Glen. You aren't calling me at two in the morning to tell me you've found the greatest woman in the world, are you?"

"Well, I have. But that's not it."

"What then?"

"Your financial worries are over."

Bob's conversation came to mind and Scott felt a chill through his body. "What? What are you talking about?"

"We hit it big, buddy. We won the big bucks." Glen was breathless with excitement.

Trying to shake the sleep from his brain, Scott said, "What big bucks?"

"Did you forget? Last week, we bought a couple of tickets on the Lotto jackpot, and we hit it. I heard the numbers on the radio. We're splitting 40 million. YEE-HAW!!!!"

Scott was stunned, and began to think he must be dreaming. "Glen, is this a joke, or are you drunk?"

"I shit you not, bro. Those bucks are all ours. I'm going to have a drink to celebrate. Tomorrow, we'll go down to the place and collect, that is after I tell the airport they can kiss my ass goodbye. Start making plans. bud. See ya in the morning." Glen hung up.

Still in a state of shock, Scott put down the phone and literally pinched himself. It hurt, so he knew he was awake and not dreaming. This would really be the end of his financial troubles. Then he had a sobering thought. *Mollie*. She would want half, at least, of his winnings. They were still legally married and she would be first in line when she found out. Scott groaned. He realized he would have to do something to stop that from happening. But what? Bob's voice popped into his head. *I'll do something for you and you can return the favour.*

"No!" Scott shouted aloud. "Get out of my head."

He slept in fits and starts for the few hours left before morning. At 7:30, Scott called and left word at the office that he wouldn't be in that day. He had barely drifted off to sleep again when the front doorbell rang. And rang. And rang. Eyes like slits, he staggered across his room and stubbed his toe on the door. He muttered and cursed all he way to the front door..

"Who's there?"

"It's me. Your millionaire friend," Glen's cheery voice called out.

"Don't you ever sleep?" Scott asked as he opened the door.

"Not on this beautiful morning. I've brought you breakfast," Glen said, waving a paper bag and two coffee containers. "Not quite the silver platter to which you will become accustomed, but will suffice to start this glorious day." He headed toward the kitchen. Scott shuffled behind.

"Tibby, my favourite kitty in the world. How are you this morning? Do you know that you will probably get a silk bed to lie in? And who knows what other fabulous kitty treats." Miss Tibbles purred and rubbed on Glen's leg. "Pretty girl," he said, petting her head.

"Glen." Scott dropped into a chair. "God, I'm still having trouble coming to grips with this."

"It's a gift from the gods, my man. So enjoy."

"Yeah, well. There is a little problem. Mollie. As soon as she hears, she's going to have her hand out." He sipped the coffee.

"Oooh...that is a bummer. Um, what can we do? Let me think, while I give this bagel a chew." With his mouth nearly full, Glen continued, "I suppose giving her half is out of the question. Although ten million is still a big chunk of change."

Scott looked at him.

"Nah, you're right. She doesn't deserve any more than she's already taken. Wait a sec." He pulled a wry mouth. "Ummm, no, that won't work."

"What?"

"I was thinking that I could claim the whole thing and then give you your half after you guys divorce, but that wouldn't work because we've both signed the ticket."

"Hmm. Hey, do you remember that guy who was sitting on the other side of me at the bar last night?"

"Sort of. I really had my eyes elsewhere." Glen raised his eyebrows and smiled.

"Right. Anyway, this jerk called me last night. He said he heard me telling you my phone number. Do you know what this guy wanted?"

"Can't imagine. You're not that good-looking." Glen chuckled.

"Idiot. He offered to kill Mollie if I would kill his wife. Like that movie, you know, Strangers on a Train, sort of thing. I couldn't believe it."

"Holy shit! I remember that movie! So what did you tell him?"

Scott looked incredulous. "What do you think I told him? I said he was nuts and I wasn't about to kill anyone. Can you imagine someone actually doing this? Maybe I should report him to the police."

"Might be an idea, although he most likely was joking ... or drunk."

"Joking or not, I don't want Mollie dead, I just want her out of my life."

"Her death would certainly do that."

Scott rolled his eyes.

Glen chuckled. "I know. I know. Get real. So ... back to the ten million dollar problem..."

"I don't see any way around it," Scott said. "And it's not so bad. Like you said, ten million is still a ton of money, and more than I ever expected to see in my lifetime."

"Giving her half is a shame, but I guess that's the only solution."

Bob's voice popped into Scott's head again. Glen's voice chased it away.

"Scott, I was thinking. Before we go down there to claim the money, maybe we should visit a financial advisor or something like that so we can figure out what to do with the huge cheques. I mean, what do you do? Walk into a bank and say please deposit 20 million bucks in my account? Besides, I know that we are likely to be bombarded with requests from everyone, probably even from people we don't know. And we should maybe go away somewhere for a while, till the uproar dies down. What do you think?"

"I hadn't thought about all that, Glen. But you're right. We need to make a plan."

They sat and talked some more about how they would handle this sudden windfall, where they would go, what they would do. It was late afternoon before they finally chose an accounting firm and set up an appointment. They agreed to meet at the lottery office the next day before seeing the accountants. Glen cautioned Scott again to keep quiet about the win until everything was settled and then left to see the newest 'greatest' woman.

Scott puttered around in the kitchen, completed kitty chores, then took a coffee into the living-room and sat down, trying to let the realization of his sudden fortune sink in. He watched Miss Tibbles climb on the window ledge to survey the neighbourhood activity.

His thoughts turned again to Mollie. *Damn, if only we had a divorce settlement in place, I wouldn't have to give her any of the money.* Again, Bob's voice echoed in his mind. Scott pushed it away. He could be very happy with ten million. And he would finally be rid of Mollie.

He put his head back and thought about the future. Perhaps he should move somewhere to a more moderate climate. He could take up scuba diving. Maybe buy a boat, do some fishing. And what about the house? Maybe he should just let Mollie have it. So much to think about.

Next morning, Scott was up early, showered, dressed and ready well ahead of the appointment time with the accountant. He decided to have an extra cup of coffee while he watched the early morning news. Miss Tibbles followed him into the living-room and sat at his feet in case a treat should be forthcoming.

"... traffic is backed up for several miles on I26, as police attempt to clear the scene of the horrific accident which claimed the life of a woman who appeared to lose control of her car and plummet over the side of the cliff. Her name has not been released, pending notification of next of kin. In other news ..."

Scott hated to look at or hear about traffic wrecks, especially when he was about to get in a car, so he gave only a cursory glance at the crumpled vehicle, a white Dodge van. *Probably something like mine. Only, of course, it isn't mine any more. It's Mollie's.*

At that moment, the over-confident mouse decided to stroll across in front of the window. Tibby went into full attack mode. She hunched down, muscles tight, then made a huge leap, landed with two paws and her big chest on the mouse.

When it didn't move, Miss Tibbles picked it up in her mouth, brought it to Scott and dropped it at his feet.

Whether the mouse died from fright or from fifteen pounds of fur landing on it, Scott wasn't sure, but he congratulated Tibby on her capture and decided that she might be useful on a boat or wherever he ended up. After ensuring there was no movement from the mouse, he put it in the garbage outside.

As he reached for the phone, it rang. It was Glen. A very subdued Glen.

"Scott, I am so sorry. Are you all right?"

"Yes, of course. I was just about to call you. Why? What's up?"

"Omigod. You haven't heard."

"Heard what?"

"Oh shit, man." Glen paused, cleared his throat. "I hate to be the one to tell you, but there was a car accident. I heard it on the radio. It was Mollie. She's dead. I'm sorry, man. I mean, I know you're separated and all that, but still ..."

"That was Mollie?" Scott was stunned and his heart seemed to stop. "What ... do they know how ... what ...?"

"Maybe I should come over. You don't sound too good."

"No. No. I'm all right. It's just a bit of a shock, you know? I'll be fine."

"Are you sure?"

"Yeah, yeah."

"Too bad, but, you know, it was really her greed that got her killed."

"What do you mean?"

"She was on her way to see you when she crashed. I know because she left a message on my voice mail earlier. She tried calling you, but was told the number had been changed, so she called me to get the new one. I wasn't home, so I guess she decided to drive over to see you."

Scott's mouth fell open and he touched his forehead. "Oh God. If only I hadn't changed the number." He groaned.

"Yes, well. Nothing you can do about it now. And it does solve the problem."

"What?"

"I don't mean to be crass, but, uh, the money's all yours now."

"Geez, you can mention that at a time like this?"

"Sorry, just being practical, bud."

"Yeah, I guess so. I was thinking about Mollie, not money."

"I understand. But life goes on and we've got to be at Johnson, Brown in an hour and a half. So ... I'll see you there?"

'"Yeah. Okay, Glen."

Scott's mind was in a whirl. He felt cold, and his hands shook. But it was an accident, right? It couldn't have had anything to do with that crazy Bob and his scheme. Or did it? The thought persisted.

The doorbell rang. Scott jumped. He opened the door to find two police officers standing there. They asked his name, introduced themselves, said they were sorry to inform him of the death of his wife in a car accident. Mollie had listed him as next of kin in her wallet. Scott explained they were separated but agreed to contact Mollie's mother, as requested. After being assured there was nothing more they could do, the policemen left.

Scott phoned Mollie's mother and listened to a five minute harangue which mostly involved expletives about his mother and Scott being a bastard and a lousy husband. She made it clear that she would make the funeral arrangements without Scott's help and that he should mind his own business and not show up anywhere.

In a cab on the way to the meeting with Glen at the accountants' office, Scott mulled over recent events. He had a dim memory, something to do with Glen hearing about Mollie on the radio. Whatever it was, it eluded him. He had other things to think about, far more interesting, such as what to do with 20 million dollars. Scott leaned back against the seat, closed his eyes and smiled as visions of tropical islands floated in his mind.

The accounting firm was very happy to meet the two men and offered multiple suggestions on where and how to place their money so that the government didn't make off with most of it.

At the conclusion of the meeting, Scott and Glen drove to the lottery office to make their claim. This turned out to be more complicated than they expected. The ticket had to be verified which, as nearly as they could determine, meant that it was put under some type of microscope to make sure it was authentic and, of course, they had to provide several pieces of identification, including a sample of their handwriting.

After having their picture taken with a dummy cheque, the happy winners received the 20 million dollar cheques and hopped into Glen's car.

"I think I'll donate this baby to a high school shop class. When I took the auto class, we were always pleased to get a real car to work on." He smiled at the memory. "If we don't move away, I would certainly buy something better than this old clunker."

"The car's not even three years old, hardly what I would call an "old clunker," Scott said.

En route to the bank, Glen suggested they should get cashier's cheques and take them to a bank in the Caymans where the money couldn't be touched by the government.

"We might as well get plane tickets before we go to the bank , and I think it would be a good idea to rent safety deposit boxes to hold everything overnight – just as a precaution."

Scott agreed. Glen pulled over to the Utopia Travel Agency. Scott's heart beat faster with excitement as he looked at the travel posters for exotic locations. They booked their seats on a flight to Grand Cayman for the next day, with an open-ended ticket so they could return whenever they were reasonably sure the furor of their win had died down.

Back in the car, the men high-fived. "The Caymans, buddy," Scott said. They let out a whoop and headed to the bank.

Scott invited Glen in for a drink when they arrived at his house, but he declined, citing the need to pack and get organized for their trip.

Scott leaned back in the car window. "I don't know how I'm going to be able to sleep tonight, Glen. My heart is still racing. Good thing I've got stuff to do to keep me busy this afternoon."

"Me too, pal. Don't forget the limo will be at your doorstep bright and early tomorrow morning."

"Never fear. I'll be ready." Scott waved his friend off and hurried into the house to get ready for his trip and make arrangements for Miss Tibbles to stay at a boarding-house for cats.

Scott microwaved a tv dinner; the ding of the microwave was followed immediately by the ring of the doorbell. He frowned. *What the hell?*

Waiting on the front porch were two policemen, and an older man in plainclothes, holding up an identification badge and card. They asked to come in and followed Scott to the living-room.

Although he had done nothing wrong, the presence of the police made him nervous. Scott's palms became damp and beads of sweat formed on his forehead. "What's this about? Mollie's accident?"

"Something like that." The man in civvies introduced himself as Detective Allen. "How long have you and your wife been separated?" he asked.

"Um, about four months, I think. But we still speak - spoke - occasionally."

"Were you getting a divorce?"

"Uh, well, yes. That was the plan. Nothing was settled yet though."

"Were you and you wife on good terms?"

"Yes, I guess you could say that, although she got annoyed with me when her cheque was late. I made an agreement to pay her $1000.00 a month until we negotiated a divorce settlement."

"That was pretty generous of you."

"I was just trying to keep the peace," Scott said.

"We also heard that you won a big lottery."

Scott was stunned. How could the word have spread so quickly. "Uh, yes. My friend and I split this week's draw. But what has that got to do with anything?"

"Well now that your wife's dead, you won't have to split it with her, will you?"

Scott felt a deep chill. "Wait a minute. What are you getting at?" His eyes widened. "Mollie had a car accident. I didn't have anything to do with that."

"Are you sure about that?"

"I don't understand. What are you talking about?"

"It wasn't an accident, Mr. Harris. The brake lines on her car had been cut. Someone wanted her dead."

"My God!!! Are you sure?" Scott felt he was choking. "But ... what ... what ... You don't think I did that, do you?"

"Ten million dollars is a pretty good motive, don't you think?"

"I didn't try to kill Mollie. I wanted her out of my life, but not that way. I planned on splitting the money with her."

"I'm afraid we're going to have to take you to the precinct for further questioning." The detective nodded to the two uniforms. They approached Scott, pulled him to his feet and handcuffed him.

"You can't do this! I've done nothing wrong! This is insane." He struggled against the arms of the policemen. "Wait! Let me call my friend."

"You can make a call from the station."

Still protesting his innocence, Scott was hustled into the patrol car, taken to the local precinct and ushered inside. They sat him at a desk on the opposite side of Detective Allen.

"You promised me I could make a call," Scott said, as he stared at Allen.

The detective shoved the phone toward him and Scott dialled Glen's number. Frantically, he explained what had happened and where he was.

"That's terrible, Scott. You'll need a lawyer, of course. Are they keeping you overnight?"

“I would imagine. They seem to want to ask me about everything I’ve ever done in my life.”

“At least you’ve got the money in the bank to get a really good lawyer.”

“Uh, sure. I guess. You’re right. I do need a good lawyer.”

“You didn’t do this, did you, Scott? I mean, you never touched her car, right?”

“Shit, Glen! How can you even say such a thing? You know me. You know I’d never hurt Mollie or anyone else.”

“All right. Don’t get excited. I just had to check, you know. Listen, I’ll get in touch with a great lawyer and we’ll come down there first thing in the morning. By the way, what did you do with your safety deposit key?”

“Oh shit! I forgot all about it. I think I left it lying on the night table when I was packing my suitcase.”

“That’s not good. What if the cops decide to search your house and find that key? They’ll look in that safety deposit box, find the plane ticket and assume you were running away.

“Oh God!”

“How about if I go and get the key for you?”

He relaxed his shoulders. “That would be great. Thanks, Glen. You’re a good friend.”

“No problem. Oh ... don’t forget to tell the cops about that guy from the bar.”

“Good idea. Thanks again. See you tomorrow then.” Scott hung up.

At the other end, Glen put down the phone and grinned.

"Afraid not," he said aloud. He patted the new plane ticket and passport in his jacket pocket. He smiled at the man with dark hair and horn-rimmed glasses who smiled back at him from the mirror. "Before morning, Mr. Charles McKenzie will be in Colombia where $40 million will buy a very nice life indeed." He laughed aloud as he placed a cap on his head. Admired his disguise one more time, picked up a cane and limped to the door

Opportunity had knocked very loudly this time.

THE END

TARA

The room is still, the air heavy with the mingled smells of flowers arranged in a horseshoe shape around the elegant coffin. I do not need to look at the photograph to remember the glorious raven hair, sparkling blue eyes, full luscious lips, for her face has haunted me for three years, filled my dreams, appeared in a thousand places... and no place. Tara, my love, my curse.

I rest my hand on the lid, aware of the reality that lies within and wonder if her face will haunt me throughout eternity or will I find peace at last.

But I get ahead of myself. My name is Richard Valentine and I am a writer. More accurately, a writer of plays, some good, some bad. A few of the good ones, and, luckily, fewer of the bad ones, have made their way to the stage in productions large and small.

My obsession with Tara began four years ago. I was sitting in the theater with the director, Paul Andracotti, watching the seemingly endless parade of hopeful actors and actresses come onto the stage and render my lines with varying degrees of talent. So far, none had the spark that both Paul and I were hoping for. Disappointed and bored with the proceedings, I stood up to stretch my long legs now cramped from sitting.

A flash of white near the back of the theater caught the corner of my eye. I turned and saw a young woman standing by the last row of seats. Although she wasn't moving, there was a luminescence about her that shimmered as I watched. Her eyes locked on mine and I couldn't help but stare. Instantly, I knew she would be perfect for the part of Lenore. I leaned towards Paul and tapped his shoulder.

"I've found Lenore. Look." When I turned back, she was gone.

Paul turned his head. "Where? You're hallucinating, buddy." He blew a large pink bubble gum circle and sucked it back into his mouth.

"She was there. Wait!" I yelled, running to the back of the theater.

I arrived at the front door in time to see her getting into a taxi which lunged forward into the mid-day traffic. My heart was pounding, reminding me that my sedentary life wasn't ideal for producing a fit body, especially in a forty year old. Janey, my second wife, had shamed me into jogging with her every day, but we'd been divorced about eight years and I had again settled comfortably into my reclusive abode surrounded by snack food, cigarettes and manuscripts. Like Connie before her, Janey hadn't been able to stand the loneliness inflicted by a man whose world was wrapped up in fictional people.

Now this fair vision had disappeared, likely forever. Sadly, I went back inside to resume viewing the cattle call.

"Did you find your mystery woman?" Paul asked, his gum-chewing not missing a beat.

"Missed her. She got into a cab."

"Right. Heh! Maybe you'd like to write a mystery play: The Case of the Vanishing Woman."

I decided to ignore Paul's remarks. This was my second time working with him and we'd clashed swords before with very little encouragement. We are so totally different. He is loud in speech, friendly and seemingly easy-going, but underneath that affable exterior is a very determined man who knows exactly what he wants and is prepared to do what it takes to get it. There is a coldness about Paul which he keeps hidden, but occasionally it flashes through the laughter like a bolt of jagged lightning. But that's not a totally bad thing. It is Paul's determination that makes his productions successful. He refuses to accept anything less than perfection from the people he works with. Including me. And God knows, I am not perfect.

As the day wore on, Paul became more and more irritable, and after selecting the two hopefuls that he would seduce in the evening, he finally ended the session.

"Why don't you get one or two of the girls and join me for dinner?"

"No thanks, Paul. I've a date with my computer."

"Why waste time looking at pictures of tits and asses on the internet when you can have the real live thing right here?"

I didn't feel like arguing with him. Actually, I felt like punching him in the face. When he's not thinking like a director, he's thinking like a whoremaster.

"Later," I said, turning to leave.

"Aw, don't be such a party pooper. You need to get out more and have a little fun. You know what they say, all work and no play makes Dickie a poor lay." He laughed heartily at his stupid joke.

I gritted my teeth, gave a short nod and left - quickly. His derisive laughter followed me out of the hall. At the front door, I lit a cigarette and inhaled gratefully. Asshole! That was the worst part of being a writer. Having to work with stupid jerks like Andracotti. Why was it that people like him always seemed to have the money while the rest of us schmucks have to work hard just to keep afloat? Hell, he was Italian - maybe he had Mafia connections.

By the time I got home, I was in no mood to work. While grabbing a beer out of the frig, a lonely egg reminded me that the shopping list was still in my pocket. No food somehow seemed a fitting end to a miserable day.

On the brink of slipping into a really foul mood, the phone rang interrupting my fall over the precipice. It was Markie, my irrepressible younger sister for whom nothing is impossible and all problems have a solution. Even older brothers who can't seem to make a relationship work.

"Rick, glad I caught you home. How are you?"

"Good. Just fine." Even to my ears, I sounded grumpy.

"You don't sound fine; you sound a little down."

"Nah, I'm all right."

"Rick, I can always tell when you're down, but I have the perfect idea to make you feel better." I groaned inwardly. "And besides, you'd be helping me out enormously. Are you free this evening?"

"Well, I, uh..."

"Great. Then puhleeze do me the favour of joining Carl and me for dinner at Fabio's. We have to entertain the Randalls - business reasons - and you know how much Carl hates Stan although he needs him for a client. And besides you've always got along well with Sandra and it would be so helpful to make things go smoother if you were there, and..."

There was almost no stopping Markie when she took flight and it's usually better just to hop on board and go along with her plans.

"Markie, whoa! All right. I'll come. What time?"

"Thanks, Rick. I knew I could count on you. Eight o'clock and don't forget to wear a tie. Oh, by the way, Stan Randall is bringing his new ..."

A sudden thought struck me. "This isn't another attempt at matchmaking, is it?"

"Of course not. It just happens that the new associate is a woman and he wants to introduce her to Carl because she's likely going to take over his agency file. It would be nice if we could have an even number for a meal. No subterfuge on my part. Honestly."

I was dubious, but a vision of the lone egg popped into my head and I agreed to go.

Everyone else was there by the time I arrived. When we were introduced, it was obvious that Victoria (Tori, for short) Marshall was just as uncomfortable as I was at this 'no ulterior motive' meeting. I gave Markie the 'stink eye', but she pretended a great interest in a ceiling fixture.

As expected, the meal was delicious, and, as also expected, Carl asked me to take Victoria home. I may be a recluse, but I am a gentleman - my parents saw to that when I was young - so I agreed.

We were able to relax a little more now that the "eyes of Texas" weren't upon us, but Tori's obvious good looks and pleasant manner could not drive away the shadow of Tara that loomed between us. I felt Tori's disappointment when I turned down her offer of a nightcap, but I think she believed the excuse that I used for every unwanted request that I received - the desperate need to finish a rewrite that was being demanded of me. At least, that is what I told myself.

Auditions continued but I managed to duck out on the majority, citing an obscure illness. I did promise to enlist the aid of everyone I knew in our search for the 'perfect' man and woman - well, perhaps not the less desirable of the acquaintances I had acquired during my early years of cheap travel throughout Europe and our own states. In truth, I was looking for Tara ... everywhere - surely a fool's errand, as my practical side kept insisting, and whose persuasiveness began to win me over.

But my luck changed the day I decided to sit on a park bench and contemplate life. For some obscure reason, a nail, unseen by me, stuck out from the side of the arm at the end of the wooden bench. As I sat down, said nail reached out and inserted itself in the sleeve of my favourite jacket and viciously tore into the material creating a tear so large that I could no longer deem myself fit to be seen in public wearing it.

Ah, blessed, cursed nail!

With nothing better to do and in no great rush to do it, I went to my favourite men's shop in pursuit of another jacket. As usual, I declined sales help and looked on the racks for something suitable. I made a selection, put it on and stepped in front of a full-length mirror. And there she was! Momentarily confused, I stared at my reflection and hers. She turned from the front counter and exited the store. In great haste, I tore off the jacket and raced after her.

The cab door was closing. I looked around frantically for another taxi, caught the attention of a driver with a face that belonged in a wrestling ring and hopped in.

"Follow that cab," I said. Instead of moving, he turned, stared at me as if I had escaped from the psychiatric ward at some hospital.

“You“re kidding me, right?”

I told him I assuredly was not kidding and pulled some money from my wallet. He turned front and pulled out into the traffic. His speed was no faster than normal in the city, which is to say, it was very fast, but I could not see the cab in which my vision was riding. To complicate matters, there now appeared at least two other taxis. Disheartened, I told the driver to stop. I handed him the money on the meter plus a reasonable tip, but he stared at me and kept his hand out. I dropped another $20. in the pile and made my exit before he locked me in.

It was close to dinner time, too late to go to the theatre, so I turned into a nearby pub for a bite to eat and a beer. In my head, I tossed around all possible ideas of why she had been in a men’s shop in the first place. The thought that she might be married was the most discouraging and I tried to push it aside. I was on my second beer when she walked in the door. With a man.

I kept an eye on them and spent so long sipping my third beer, that the waitress began to give me weird looks. I smiled lamely at her and said I was waiting for someone. She nodded understanding and left me alone.

The couple finally finished their meal and paid their bill. I hastily threw down some cash to cover mine and followed them out the door. He drove a flashy red sports car. I hated him. But it did make him easy to follow in yet another cab whose driver was obviously excited to be part of a subversive (in his opinion) operation.

The sports car disappeared into the underground parking lot of an expensive condominium building. I made note of the address and had my driver take me home.

The next morning, I parked my car outside what I hoped was her building. She appeared around 10 am and walked down the street toward a Starbucks. Coffee sounded good to me and I squished the thought she might emerge with a take-out. I waited five minutes then entered. Her mint green jacket was easy to spot and I took my coffee to a table several feet away. I was about to light up when I remembered the 'No Smoking' rule. I like a cigarette with my coffee.

About twenty minutes later, Miss X made a call on her cell. I hoped she wasn't calling the sports car. She wasn't. A cab pulled up out front and she left the café, with me hot on her heels - or I would have been if I hadn't stumbled over a chair and righted myself by grabbing the shoulder of a guy who looked less than happy about being used for a grab bar.

I raced to my car, made an illegal U-turn and followed after the taxi. Her destination was a large, classy department store located in the heart of the city. What that means is nowhere to park except an underground lot. But I was determined. Ticket properly placed near the window of the dash, I found a space and hurried to the elevator. The obvious choice for a woman in a department store would be the ladies clothing department and that's where I headed. I spotted her checking out dresses, with the help of a svelte young woman. I acted nonchalant as I made my way - very slowly - down a rack of spring coats.

When I rejected the assistance of the second salesperson who approached me, I saw her make a phone call. Shortly after, a muscular suit arrived and checked me out. As he came toward me, I guessed that my time in ladies wear was over, and as casually as I could, I made my way toward the elevators. The suit followed, pointed at me and with a downward motion of his arm, indicated I should take my depraved self down, while his hitchhiker's thumb told me to get out of the store. He waited until the doors closed behind me.

It seemed my investigation was over for the day, but not forever. I continued following her on the days she left the condo, and tried to figure how I could make myself known to her.

After two weeks, common sense prevailed, I figured it was time to join the gum-chewing Andracotti and see what was happening with rehearsals.

He chewed off my head, of course, and I fielded his questions with a story of being indisposed for digestive reasons. He wasn't happy with the explanation, but let it go in favour of bringing me up-to-date on the business at hand. As it turned out, of the eight characters in the play, he had cast six, but the roles of Lenore and Arthur were still without satisfactory actors. I started to wish that Paul weren't so demanding and had to remind myself that this is why his productions succeeded.

My second day back was half over when an actor, Josh Winslow, read for us and won the lead role. He was perfect, almost as good as I would have been ten years ago. Yes, I was an actor before I started writing.

While Andracotti wrote down Josh's details, I skipped outside for a smoke. I was leaning against the building, my mind wandering, when a voice spoke beside me.

"Got a light?"

I reached in my pocket for my lighter and turned to face the owner of the sultry voice. My hand froze against the metal. My eyes opened wide and I wowed her with my eloquent, intelligent greeting.

"Oh! It's you!"

She laughed, a sound so melodious, the gods were surely enchanted. "Yes. The last time I checked anyway."

I stood there as if mesmerized, and perhaps, in truth, I was. The raven hair, delightful smile and eyes blue as the Caribbean Sea surely held me spellbound.

She leaned her head toward her right arm, still bent up from the elbow, holding a cigarette. "A light?" She raised her eyebrows quizzically.

My eyes blinked and I realized what a fool I must look.

"Sorry. Of course." She held my hand steady, put her cigarette to the flame. She looked sideways at me and straightened up.

"Richard. Me." *God, was there no end to my bumbling?* "I mean, my name's Richard Valentine."

"Me. Not Jane."

She laughed aloud and, sporting a red face, I joined her.

A grin still played around those luscious lips when she said, "I'm Tara."

She saw my surprise. "Yes, like the plantation in Gone With The Wind. My mother was a big fan." She chuckled. "London."

"London? As in England?"

"Right. My name, not birthplace."

I smiled and nodded my head. Not only beautiful but with a sense of humour, as well. Never particularly good with the spoken word or small talk, I shuffled one foot back and forth, wondering how to say that I'd love to have her in the lead role of my play, without sounding like a version of the old Hollywood couch routine. As it happened, she took the matter out of my hands.

She looked me right in the eye. "Why have you been following me, Mr. Valentine?"

Busted! And flustered and sheepish. My words came out in a rush. "Oh, uh, sorry, uh ... well, the truth is, I saw you standing in the back of the theatre and I want you, er, would like you to have the lead role in my play that is just being cast, but then you disappeared and I didn't know how to approach you with that suggestion because you might think I was a ... um ... trying to get you ... um, well you know," I finished lamely.

"So you thought being a stalker was a better choice?"

"I wasn't stalking you, I was ..." I realized I had no place else to go. "Okay, I guess I was stalking you - but in a good way. At least my intentions were good."

Tara never took her eyes off me throughout my whole miserable explanation. She waited a few seconds before speaking.

"Relax, Mr. Valentine. I've seen your plays and although I'm not an actress, I would love to try out for the lead role in your new one."

"Great!" I nodded to the front doors beside us. "We should go in now and talk to Paul Andracotti. He's auditioning and directing."

We put out our cigarettes, went to the door, and as she walked through, she said, "By the way - I've never been inside this theatre before."

So happy was I, her comment washed over my head, after making the briefest stop at Port Puzzlement. It was a portent but I was unaware.

I called out to Paul who was talking to one of the hopefuls. He did a double-take when he saw Tara. I introduced them, and he was almost salivating, something I discovered quite often happened when a man met Tara.

From the moment Tara walked on stage, she owned it, even though there was little on it other than a nondescript backdrop. She had read a scant two lines when Paul jumped to his feet and announced Tara had the part of Lenore. Josh Winslow looked as surprised as I felt, but he closed the script for Arthur and offered his congratulations. I heard him say, "I'm looking forward to working with you." He wasn't the only one.

Paul Andracotti's testosterone went into overdrive. At every opportunity, he went onstage to give her up close and personal directions. Everyone else was barked at from his front row seat. Much as he tried to insert himself into her personal life by way of dinner invitations and offers to escort her to this or that shindig, she steadfastly refused. The reason, although it took him a while to figure it out, was that she preferred me. Me.

I had difficulty believing it when I was away from her, which was often, as there were things she had to do, among which was preparing for the part and once underway, there were performances. Ah yes, there were performances and I attended them all.

The play was a smash hit, in no small way thanks to Tara. She was magnificent! Throngs of hangers-on, notables and well-wishers crowded her dressing-room nightly after the performance. Tara thrived on the adulation, and I cannot blame her. I made it a point to wait until most of the crowd had gone. Tara and I would go out for a late supper and she often had to wade through numbers of autograph hounds. I would stand and wait, proud to be seen with this beautiful lady.

Still, from time to time we managed to have quiet dinners and lunches away from curious eyes. My life had soared to heights I did not believe existed. Between the success of my play and Tara's love - and yes, she professed her love for me many times when we were alone - I was in seventh heaven. Certainly she flirted at parties and social gatherings, but I believed it was harmless, at least for nearly a year, until the doubts began to grow like a rolling snowball.

The changes were subtle and crept in as quietly as a snake approaching its victim. There would be excuses of tiredness, obscure appointments. We never lived together and there were times I would arrive at her luxurious condo to find her not home or 'indisposed', according to her maid.

For a few months, I was more than willing to give her the benefit of any doubt I had until those doubts overpowered my ability to concentrate on the writing of a new play, something which was intended to showcase Tara in the lead role.

The bubble burst just before the play was ready to close for two months to give the actors a much-needed break. I decided to surprise Tara with a luxury two-week cruise around Italy and the Greek Islands, followed by three weeks in a suite I had rented on the Italian Riviera. Several days before we were to depart, I was invited to dinner by my irrepressible sister, Markie, who suggested that I bring Tara. I agreed to meet them at a fashionable supper club at eight.

I called Tara to relay the invitation. She apologized profusely, but said she had a major migraine and could not get out of bed. I was disappointed but went ahead to meet Carl and Markie. We had barely finished our salads when Tara walked in ... with Josh Winslow. I tried to cover my embarrassment while the other two pretended not to see.

The food was good, but I had little appetite. Surreptitious glances at Tara and Josh resulted in seeing them clink wine glasses and touch each other in what appeared to be a familiar and loving gesture.

I was stunned. Josh Winslow! Impossible! I had met his girlfriend. My mind flew in several directions. Obviously there was some kind of mistake. I was confused, angry and yes, very angry. Had I been cuckolded all these months?

Early the next day, I went to the theatre and waited in her dressing-room. Startled, Tara jerked backwards when she opened the door and saw me, but she quickly recovered.

"Darling! How lovely to see you."

Her silky green dress rustled as she came to me and kissed my cheek. Before she could turn completely away, I took hold of her shoulders and spun her back.

"You're hurting me." Wide-eyed, she searched my face. "Whatever's wrong?"

Doubt flashed into my mind and I dropped my hands. "Oh. Sorry. I just ... how's your migraine?"

"Oh it's much better, darling. Thank goodness." Tara stepped behind the privacy screen, emerged a moment later wearing a housecoat and went to her dressing-table.

Hoping for the truth, I asked the question which was burning in my mind. "Did you rest in bed last evening?

She started pinning up her hair. "Yes. I didn't move a muscle all night."

A brief knock on the door was followed by the entry of Tara's dresser, a no-nonsense lady who told me it was time to leave. As I headed to the door, Tara called out. "Aren't you gong to wish me luck, darling?"

"Yes, of course." I walked back and kissed her on the cheek. "Break a leg."

She smiled. "Such an odd expression I always think."

I nodded and left the room. Tara lied! The hurt exploded in a raging anger. She had made a fool of me! I slammed out of the theatre and went home to seek the comfort of Jack Daniels. Rather than soothing, Jack added fuel to the fire that burned within me. I paced the floor, a million thoughts tumbling about like sand in a desert storm ... thoughts that grew darker with each glass of whiskey.

Forty-eight hours passed during which I ignored the ringing phone and door-knocking. Forty-eight hours including the ten minute phone call which I will regret to my dying day.

I had just finished dressing when a great banging started on the door, followed by Paul yelling my name and demanding I open up immediately. I obliged.

He stormed through, raging worse than any major hurricane. I fully expected him to have a heart attack or his head to explode like a volcano. From the rush of expletives flowing like lava, I gathered he was furious with everyone in our little world. I waited until his rant died down and asked him to explain his problem in something other than swear words.

In a rush of words, Paul said he couldn't locate Josh Winslow to negotiate a contract with him - guessed he had gone back to his family in France - nor Tara to ask if she knew where Josh was, he'd had to put the understudies on at the last minute, on top of that, I hadn't answered my phone or the door for nearly two days and how the hell was he supposed to do his job when everyone kept disappearing.

I casually made the suggestion that they had just gone away together. Another torrent of words poured forth during which I discovered he thought my parents hadn't been married, I had an IQ of a fly, and I believed he was an idiot.

Paul eyed the empty bottles of Jack Daniels and said it was obvious what I had been doing. I could hardly deny it as the evidence was right there.

He laughed at my suggestion that Josh and Tara had decided to take a little holiday somewhere, but in view of no other idea coming to mind, Paul agreed to wait another day to see if they came back.

With no sign of them the next day, Paul urged me to come with him to the police station to file a missing persons report. It was obvious by the way the officer took our information he believed they had gone off to do what couples do when they disappear together.

The next two days, during which I cancelled my cruise and suite reservations, dragged by. The play closed and Paul called the police again, but they had nothing to report. Although I found it difficult to concentrate, I resumed writing the new play with a modicum of success.

Shortly after that, I received a call from the Global Travel Agency asking for Tara. The agent was taken aback when I told her that Tara was missing.

"I'm Rick Valentine. What's this about and why are you calling here?"

Her confusion was obvious from her search for words. "I … I … we had expected Miss London in to pick up the tickets, but when she didn't come … er, one of them is in your name, so I decided to call … you … er, I understand it was to be a surprise … I don't want to, er …"

"What was a surprise? You'd best tell me whatever you know."

"Right. Well, we had been working with Miss London and Mr. Winslow to arrange a yearly lease on Mr. Winslow's family villa on the French Riviera. This has taken a long time for a variety of reasons, primarily due to Mr. Winslow's uncle being ill and unable to sign the papers. Confirmation of the lease arrived three days ago and after that we booked flights for Miss London and Mr. Valentine, leaving next week. We've been trying to reach her, but with no success, and I finally decided to call you, although she was very adamant about this being a surprise for you."

I was speechless. I tried to absorb what the agent had said. *Mr Valentine and Miss London? His family villa in France. A surprise for me?* My world turned upside-down and shattered into a million pieces.

"Mr. Valentine?"

"Yes, yes, I'm here. I … I'm afraid Miss London and Mr. Winslow have disappeared. I, uh, we have no idea where they are. All I can suggest is that you cancel all those arrangements. I'm sorry."

"Oh dear. I ... uh ... yes, yes we will. Um, I'm very sorry for your ... that Miss London is missing."

My mind was awhirl. All those excuses were just Tara trying to arrange a surprise for me? I collapsed on the couch and covered my face with my hands. I was devastated. *Why didn't I trust her? Why didn't I just ask? Oh God - she LOVED me! And I ... I ...*

My torment was such that I could not sleep or eat. I wish I could have killed myself, but I had not the strength. Time passed - I have no idea of how much or how little.

I guess it was Paul who pulled me back from the brink of insanity. I was sitting on the couch when he walked in.

"You look like hell," he said.

I had no answer. He was probably right.

"When's the last time you ate?"

I shrugged my shoulders. I had no idea.

"Get your ass into the bathroom and get cleaned up. We've got things to do. I'll order in some food."

Apparently, I didn't move fast enough, because he pulled me to my feet and literally shoved me down the hall to the bathroom. By the time I had finished, the house smelled of chicken and fries, and my stomach rumbled. I couldn't manage a lot, but while I was eating, Paul told me that he had contacted various friends around the globe asking them to search for Tara and that her photo was circulating on social media sites. He leaned back on my couch, looking worried.

"I've had no results from anything. It looks like she's just vanished from the face of the earth. Josh, too. Wherever they are, they must be together."

I agreed with him.

My global friends were also contacted for a different reason this time, and for more than a year we waited for news, hope diminishing with each passing week. Life went on, but there was a huge gap in mine.

Writing became a chore because I couldn't concentrate. My cigarette and alcohol bill increased to prohibitive amounts and Markie, sweet sister that she is, took me to task over my excess. Like all drinkers, I promised to stop killing whatever brain cells I had left. Paul took turns yelling and coaxing me to start writing again. For some reason, he was anxious to direct another play, perhaps because he had made a bundle on the first.

One afternoon about three months ago, my doorbell rang. When I peered through the glass, I saw a scruffy young man looking up and down the street. His demeanor gave me pause. After hesitating a moment, I yanked open the door. He jumped as if a shot had been fired by his feet.

After ascertaining that I was indeed Richard Valentine, he pressed a crumpled note into my hand, said it was from someone named Marcel, and sprinted back to a waiting cab. They sped off before I had the scrap of paper straightened out. The note was cryptic, nothing but an address in, of all places, Casablanca. I looked for inspiration in the direction the car had taken, but it was long gone. Hope sprang to life. Was there a chance Tara had been found?

I called Paul to see what he thought. After discarding all other possibilities, we decided this had to have something to do with Tara. As Paul was swimming in a sea of stage directions, he suggested I call the police who had been involved in the search for Tara. I did and they strongly advised me against paying any attention to the note. Of course, I did the only reasonable thing and immediately called to make flight arrangements to Mohammed V International Airport.

The travel agent tried to change my mind, citing the always-present possibility of a terrorist attack, mugging or something even more deadly. I finally persuaded her that I wanted to go, she booked the ticket and a hotel for me. I promised to pick up the tickets the next day, prior to departure that evening. I threw a few items into a backpack, small enough to satisfy the requirements of any airline and tried to sleep.

The overnight flight from JFK to Casablanca was uneventful and although I did manage to sleep a little, I was pretty tired when we deplaned. There were plenty of taxis waiting to take arrivals the 35 km to Casablanca proper and the Kenzi Basma Hotel. I registered with the front desk, and went to my room, happy I had arranged to have the room held for me. Despite being tired, it took me a while to fall asleep as various scenarios of what I might find floated through my mind.

It was late afternoon before I was able to shake off the tender bonds of Morpheus. After a shower and shave, I headed for the dining-room where I tried a few different dishes comprised of items unfamiliar to me but all of which were rich, spicy and excellent.

After getting in the taxi, I attempted to pronounce the name of the street - apparently not well, judging by the shrug of the driver's shoulders. I handed him the paper. He stared at it a long while before turning to look at me.

He shook his head. "No. Not go," he pointed at me. """You no go. Bad place."

I nodded my head. "Yes. Go. I want to go there."

He continued shaking his head, but when I insisted, he muttered a great spiel in what I assumed to be Arabic, gave a resigned shrug of his shoulders and pulled out into traffic.

The taxi stopped in front of a dingy hotel, its appearance not enhanced by the poor street lighting and litter carelessly thrown about. Two men in nondescript clothing stood by the wall, each with a cigarette in one hand. One of the men held a bottle of whiskey. The driver turned around and looked at me. "Bad place."

I must admit I agreed with him, but having come this far, I determined not to be dissuaded. I gave him the Dirhams and asked if he would wait for me. He half-nodded, but as soon as I was out of the cab, he took off.

The smell of the ocean mingled with the scent of cigarettes and booze. The men eyed me and I grew uncomfortable, but decided to face them head on. I showed them the paper and one of them thumbed to the building to the right of the hotel.

I couldn't decide if it was a walk-up or simply a house, but climbed the stairs, glanced back once and discovered the two men had disappeared. I shrugged my shoulders and knocked. The door was opened by a young man with several tattoos on his arms. I showed him the paper and asked if I had the right place. He took the paper, said nothing, nodded for me to step in. I brushed past and stepped into a hall lit by a bulb inside a round ball fixture that was half full of dead flies.

The door closed and I felt a hard jab in my back. The only gun I'd ever had shoved in my back was during a play. This felt like the same thing, but I was pretty sure it wasn't a stage prop, especially when a gruff voice told me to raise my hands. A hard shove in the back encouraged me to move forward and into a room to my left. I was greeted by a bright light shining into my eyes. The gun was moved to the back of my head and I was frisked down by unseen hands. My wallet and passport were taken from my pocket.

The light was removed from my eyes and I stood blinking, trying to adjust to the low lighting.

"What's your name?" a man's voice said.

I knew they had my I.D., but decided not to point out the obvious. "Richard Valentine."

"What are you doing here?"

"I'm not sure. That note was given to me at my door in New York and I decided to come in case ... it ..."

"Who sent it?"

"Uh, all I know is the man who delivered said Marcel sent it, but I don't know who that is."

To my relief, the pressure of the gun disappeared. and I slowly lowered my arms. I could now see that I was in a room with dilapidated furniture - sofa and chair. A medium height, muscular man wearing a dark jacket and pants stood against the far wall. The young man with the tattoos stepped out from behind me. I noticed he had tucked the gun into his belt.

The man moved away from the wall. "I'm Marcel," he said, extending his hand. "Sorry for the rough treatment, but we have to take precautions."

"What's this all about? Who are you?"

"We're part of a small group who rescue women and girls from slavery in certain countries. I can't go into details because our work is covert, for obvious reasons. Your name was mentioned by someone we found not too far from a compound we were about to breach, and we assumed you might know her."

My heart leapt into my throat. *She's alive! Redemption?* "Tara?"

"We don't know. We believe she attempted to escape on her own, apparently not for the first time, judging by ... er, there were certain conditions ... I must warn you, if you know her, I am sure she is very much changed from the last time you saw her."

We went to a room further down the hall. Marcel unlocked the door and looked at me. "Are you ready?"

I nodded, but there was no way in the world I could ever have been ready to see what was waiting for me.

Light from a bare bulb in a wall sconce cast shadows around the room whose emptiness was disturbed only by a bed with a chair beside it. A small lump in the bed indicated an occupant. Marcel approached, spoke quietly and drew down the sheet.

She lay on her side, raw back exposed, one small hand by her face, the other draped across her waist. Although I had been warned, I know the shock showed on my face as I took in the bruised and battered arm and legs, and when she turned her eyes to look up at me, I couldn't speak. Tears rolled down my cheeks.

"I'm afraid we couldn't do much to clean her up because of her injuries," Marcel said. "A doctor did put the cast on her arm and address the lashes on her back. We believe they were her punishment for trying to escape. They beat her badly and left her for dead in the alley."

"R - Rick," she whispered.

"Oh Tara. My darling." Where her lustrous hair had been, there was only cut and scraped scalp. Hollow cheeks, swollen jaw and black eyes replaced the beautiful face I knew and loved.

"There's one other thing. The body of a young man was washed up at the harbour the same day we found the young woman. We couldn't claim him due to all the publicity, but I wonder if you ..."

"It's possible I might know who he was. Josh Winslow and Tara disappeared at the same time."

"I just wondered. He also was badly beaten, but as I said, we can lay no claim on the body, so he will be cremated without identification."

"I understand."

"You need to get her out of here right away. We are constantly on the move and if they get wind of the fact that her body wasn't found ... let's just say you'd better leave quickly. You cannot take her on a commercial airliner. We have a jet ready to take both of you back to the US. There will be no authorities asking questions when you land. A car waits outside. Be careful when you pick her up."

I lifted her gently and Marcel slipped a blanket underneath. She moaned when I wrapped it around her and picked her up, but there was nothing I could do. As I found out later, her entire body was covered in bruises, cuts, cigarette burns and welts. We were hurried into the car, and Marcel dismissed my thanks with a wave of his hand. I cradled her until we reached our destination, a small airport somewhere outside Casablanca proper.

Tara slept through the seven hour trip, which was a blessing for both of us as she needed it, and I was not yet in control of my feelings which ranged from sorrow to anger and back again. She had been gone a year. I wondered what else she had endured during that time.

Back home, I lay Tara on my bed. She groaned and her eye fluttered open.

"Rick?" A couple of tears rolled slowly down her bruised cheek.

"Shhhh. It's okay. You're all right now. I'm going to get a doctor."

"Wait." Her voice, although hoarse and feeble, had a degree of urgency to it.

Gingerly, I touched the side of her head. "What is it?" I leaned closer.

"Josh ... don't know what ... he ... they ... separated ..."

"Don't talk any more, darling. You need to conserve your strength."

Her voice was halting. "Must ... taxi took us wrong place ... needle. Rick ... sold ... raped, tried ... escape ... I ..." Pain radiated from her eyes. I took hold of the hand she tried to lift to my face and kissed it gently, my tears falling like rain. "Love ... you ..." She went limp.

I dialled a doctor friend who lived nearby and asked him to hurry over. He was there in five minutes, looked at my face and followed me into the bedroom. He could not conceal his shock when he saw Tara. He glanced quickly at me as he placed a hand on her carotid artery. We both knew even before he put a stethoscope on her gaunt chest. My beautiful Tara was gone.

My hand that rests on the coffin lid grows icy as I remember the frail shell of my darling Tara that lies within. A voice inside my head insists that I look again at the ravages I have wrought. I resist, but something unseen grips my hand and forces me to raise the lid and face the horrific consequence of my jealousy. An eternity goes by before my hand is freed.

I close the lid quickly, but it is too late.

No longer will I be able to remember the beauty that once was. The vision of the horror is now seared in my brain. This is my punishment.

THE END